Detective Sam

The Mysterious Murder of Selena Martin

NAHK RARSI

DEDICATION

To my family, friends, colleagues and students who have always
supported me in all phases of my life

ABOUT THE AUTHOR

An Entrepreneur, Philanthropist, Researcher, Professor, Lecturer, Author, Inspirational Motivational and Professional Industrial speaker, having a total of 25+ years of experience in various professional fields.

A person who loves to donate time, experience, skills and talent to help creating a better world.

Passion for demystifying complex technical concepts led me to write books on computers, management and business topics.

Also written books on other genres for modern era.

Enjoy mentoring aspiring leaders, creating videos and teaching on YouTube channel, writing on social media and speaking at technology conferences around the world.

https://nahkrarsi.wordpress.com/

THE MYSTERIOUS MURDER OF
SELENA MARTIN

Detective Sam Taylor stepped into the small studio apartment, his eyes adjusting to the dim lighting.

He was a tall, ruggedly handsome man in his mid-30s, with a strong jawline and piercing blue eyes. His dark hair was cut short, and his sharp jawline was accentuated by a scruff of stubble. He wore a crumpled suit, a badge on his belt, and a gun holstered at his hip.

As he entered the studio, Sam's trained eyes scanned the room, taking in every detail.

He noticed the faint scent of turpentine and oil paints lingering in the air, mingling with the acrid smell of death.

His gaze landed on the lifeless body of Selena Martin, a 28-year-old artist, lying on the worn wooden floor.

Sam's eyes narrowed as he took in the scene.

Selena's eyes were frozen in a permanent stare, her skin pale and clammy. A single droplet of blood trickled from the corner of her mouth, forming a tiny crimson pool on the floor. Her legs were splayed at an awkward angle, as if she had fallen or been pushed.

Sam's gaze swept across the room, taking in the scattered art supplies: paintbrushes, canvases, and tubes of color.

He noticed a half-finished canvas on the easel, a vibrant splash of color amidst the dull, gray morning light.

The colors seemed to pulse with energy, as if Selena's creative spirit still lingered.

The victim's friend, June, had reported Selena missing yesterday evening.

She had been worried when Selena failed to show up for their planned dinner date.

The police found Selena's body this morning when June arrived at the studio to check on her.

As Sam examined the crime scene, he noticed a small notebook on the table beside Selena's easel.

The cover was worn and dog-eared. It was filled with sketches of abstract shapes and vibrant colors.

Some pages were scribbled with notes.

Sam stopped at one note which read

Selena's Notebook

Feeling lost in my own art.

I'm not good enough.

The critics don't understand me.

Sam recognized the desperation and self-doubt in those words.

He had seen similar struggles in his own life, particularly after his father's sudden passing a few years ago.

Selena's words resonated with him on a personal level and felt the connection immediately.

He turned to the next page and found a more recent entry:

Selena's Notebook

Met someone last night.

He said I'm talented, that my art is unique.

He wants to help me take it to the next level.

A red flag went off in Sam's mind.

Who was this person?

Is this person connected with Selena's murder?

Sam decided to focus on Selena's last days leading up to her death. He asked himself:

What did she do yesterday evening? Was it a robbery gone wrong or something more sinister?

He glanced around the studio again, taking note of a small folder on the table labeled "Sunshine Art Gallery".

Inside, he found a rejection letter from a prestigious gallery, stating that they were not interested in showcasing her work.

Sam felt a pang of sympathy for Selena. It seemed like she was struggling with more than just her art.

As he continued to process the scene, Sam's mind began to wander back to his own past.

His father, a detective himself, had always told him that every case started with understanding the victim's story.

Sam realized that understanding Selena's struggles could be key to solving her murder.

With his notebook and pen at hand, Sam began to take notes:

Notes

Victim: Selena Martin

Age: 28

Cause of death: Unknown

Manner of death: Homicide

Last seen alive: Yesterday evening

Suspects: Unknown

Detective Sam Taylor sat at his desk, sipping his coffee, as he delved deeper into Selena Martin's online presence.

Her social media accounts were private, but with a court order, he managed to gain access to her Facebook and Instagram profiles.

The first thing that caught his attention was a post from three days ago, where Selena had announced that she was taking a break from social media due to feeling overwhelmed and anxious.

She had mentioned struggling with the constant pressure to produce new art and the lack of recognition in the art world.

Sam's eyes scanned through her posts, searching for any clues.

He noticed that she had recently interacted with an account called "Artistic Hub", a page that shared articles and tutorials on art techniques.

The account's bio read: "Sharing the beauty of art and helping others unlock their creative potential".

Sam's gut told him that this might be a promising lead.

He requested access to the account's administrator information and began to dig deeper.

Sam couldn't find relevant information to this case.

Meanwhile, he decided to pay a visit to Selena's family home, hoping to learn more about her personal life.

Her mother, Jasmine, answered the door, her eyes red from crying.

"Please, detective, find out who did this to my daughter," she begged.

Sam introduced himself and asked if he could take a look around the house.

Jasmine led him to Selena's room, where Sam found a stack of diaries and notebooks on the nightstand.

As he flipped through the pages, he discovered a deep sense of vulnerability and self-doubt.

Selena had been struggling with anxiety and depression for

years, often feeling like she was living in the shadow of her successful parents.

Her father was a renowned artist, art dealer and businessman, and her mother was a successful businesswoman too.

On checking Selena's diary, one entry in particular caught his attention:

Selena's Notebook

I feel like I'm stuck in this rut.

My art is not good enough, my parents are always critical...

I wish I could just be myself without being judged.

Sam felt a pang of sadness and frustration. It seemed like Selena was struggling with so many pressures from all sides.

As he continued reading, he noticed that Selena had been taking antidepressants for years.

There were also mentions of therapy sessions and self-help books.

It was clear that she was trying to cope with her struggles.

The diary entries also revealed that Selena had been seeing someone new, someone who had encouraged her to keep creating art despite the criticism.

She had mentioned meeting him at an art exhibit several months ago.

Sam made a mental note to investigate this new acquaintance further.

Detective Sam Taylor sat in the Martin family's living room, surrounded by the comfortable trappings of middle-class comfort.

Jasmine, Selena's mother, sat across from him, her eyes red from crying.

"I want to know what happened to my daughter," she said, her voice trembling.

Sam nodded sympathetically. "We're doing everything we can to find out. Can you tell me more about Selena's life? Any enemies or conflicts she might have had?"

Jasmine hesitated before speaking. "Selena was always a sensitive soul. She struggled with anxiety and depression, and it affected her relationships. She had a few close friends, but they were all going through their own struggles."

Sam pulled out his notebook and began to take notes. "Who were these friends?"

"June was her closest friend. They met in art school and have been inseparable ever since. Then there was... Owen. He was an artist she met at an exhibit a few months ago. He was charming and encouraging, but... I don't know if he was good for her."

Sam's ears perked up at the mention of Owen. He made a mental note to look into him further.

Jasmine continued, "And then there was her brother, Daniel. He's a few years older than Selena and always felt responsible for her. He was... overprotective, sometimes."

Sam scribbled some more notes. "Did Daniel have any issues with Selena?"

Jasmine hesitated again before speaking. "He was always worried about her getting hurt or getting too close to someone who wasn't good for her. He could be... intense."

Sam sensed that there was more to the story, but he didn't press the issue.

As he left the Martin home, Sam felt like he had uncovered some crucial information.

He decided to pay a visit to June and Daniel to get their sides of the story.

He arrived at June's apartment, where she greeted him with tears in her eyes. "I miss Selena so much," she said.

Sam took out his notebook again. "Can you tell me more about your relationship with Selena? Were there any fights or conflicts?"

June shook her head. "We never fought, Sam. We were each other's rock. But... I did notice that she was struggling lately. She seemed distant and withdrawn."

Sam noted and thanked June for her time and headed to Daniel's apartment next.

As he walked in, Daniel looked up from his book, his eyes narrowing slightly. "What do you want?"

Sam flashed his badge. "I'm investigating Selena's murder, Daniel. Can you tell me more about your relationship with your sister?"

Daniel snorted. "I loved Selena, but she was my sister. I wanted what was best for her."

Sam sensed a hint of defensiveness in Daniel's tone.

Detective Sam Taylor sat down across from Daniel Martin; his eyes locked on the suspect's defensive posture. "Daniel, I know you loved your sister, but I need to ask some tough questions. Can you tell me where you were on the night of Selena's murder?"

Daniel shifted uncomfortably in his seat. "I was... out with friends. We went to a bar and then to a movie. I didn't get home until late."

Sam raised an eyebrow. "Can anyone confirm this alibi?"

Daniel hesitated before speaking. "I don't think so. My friends were all out of town, and I didn't think it was a big deal. But... I did talk to someone on the phone around 10 pm."

Sam's gut told him that Daniel was hiding something. "Who did you talk to?"

Daniel's eyes darted around the room before settling back on Sam. "It was... June. She was worried about Selena and wanted to know if I'd heard from her that day."

Sam's mind racing, he pulled out his notebook again. "June said you were overprotective of Selena. Did you ever feel like you were holding her back?"

Daniel's expression turned cold. "I was just trying to help her. She was so vulnerable and lost without our parents' guidance."

Sam sensed a deep-seated insecurity in Daniel's words. He decided to push further.

"Did you ever feel jealous of Selena's talent? Did you resent her for being the favored child?"

Daniel's face turned red with anger. "Of course not! Selena was my sister, and I loved her no matter what."

Sam detected a hint of defensiveness in Daniel's tone. He made a mental note to investigate further into Daniel's motives and alibi.

As he left the apartment, Sam felt like something was not right.

He decided to pay a visit to June again, hoping she might be willing to share more information.

Detective Sam Taylor sat at his desk, flipping through Selena's notebook.

Her handwriting was messy, but her thoughts were vivid.

He found an entry from a few weeks ago:

Selena's Notebook

I feel so trapped.

Like I'm drowning in my own thoughts.

I want to scream, but no one understands me.

I'm stuck in this never-ending cycle of sadness and anxiety.

Why can't I just be happy like everyone else?

Sam's heart went out to Selena. He could feel her desperation and frustration.

He decided to investigate her therapy sessions to see if there were any signs of unusual behavior or suspicious activities.

He arrived at the therapist's office and introduced himself. "I'm Detective Sam Taylor. I'm investigating the murder of Selena Martin. Can you tell me more about her therapy sessions?"

The therapist, Dr. Nelson, nodded sympathetically. "Selena was a bright and talented young woman, but she struggled with severe depression and anxiety. She came to see me regularly for several years."

Sam pulled out his notebook again. "Can you tell me more about her progress? Did she ever mention any specific fears or concerns?"

Dr. Nelson hesitated before speaking. "Selena did have some... unusual fears. She was terrified of being forgotten, like she would disappear and no one would remember her existence. It was an irrational fear, but it was deeply ingrained."

Sam's eyes narrowed. This fear seemed relevant to the case.

Dr. Nelson continued, "She also struggled with trust issues. She had trouble forming close relationships and was always worried that people would abandon her."

Sam made a note of this as well.

Detective Sam Taylor sat at his desk, staring at Selena's social media accounts on his computer screen.

He scrolled through her Instagram feed, looking for any clues that might shed light on her thoughts and feelings before her murder.

He landed on a post from a few months ago:

I feel like I'm losing myself in the crowd. Like I'm just a faceless soul in a sea of faces. I wish someone could see me, really see me.

Sam felt a pang of sadness. Selena's words were hauntingly familiar.

He wondered if this feeling of being lost and invisible might be connected to her fears of being forgotten.

He continued scrolling, searching for any other clues.

He found a post from a few weeks ago:

I'm so tired of being nice to people who don't care about me.
I'm tired of pretending to be okay when I'm dying inside.
I wish someone would understand me, really understand me.

Sam's eyes widened as he read the post again.

This seemed like a cry for help, a plea for someone to notice her pain.

He made a note to look into Selena's friends and acquaintances, to see if anyone had noticed any changes in her behavior or mood recently.

Detective Sam Taylor sat down with June again, his eyes searching for any signs of deception.

"June, I need to ask you something," he said gently. "You mentioned that you talked to Daniel on the night of Selena's murder. Can you tell me more about that conversation?"

June hesitated before speaking. "I was worried about Selena. She had been distant and withdrawn lately, and I hadn't heard from her all day. I was trying to reach out and make sure she was okay."

Sam's eyes narrowed. "And what did Daniel say?"

June's expression turned nervous. "He told me that he hadn't heard from her either, but he was going to look for her. He said she might have gone out with friends or something."

Sam's gut told him that June was hiding something. "Did you believe him?"

June shook her head. "No... I don't know what to believe. Daniel can be... intense, and I've seen him get angry with Selena before."

Sam made a mental note to investigate further into Daniel's behavior around Selena.

As he left June's apartment, Sam decided to pay a visit to Owen. Hoping he might be willing to share more information.

But before that he thought to have a word with Daniel again.

Meanwhile, Sam checked Selena's diary for any clues.

Selena's Notebook

I've been feeling so lost lately.

Daniel is always watching me, making sure I'm doing what he thinks is best for me.

But what about what I want? What about my art?

June says I'm talented, but Daniel just says I'm wasting my time.

I finally worked up the courage to tell Daniel that I'm leaving school.

He was furious, of course.

Says I'm abandoning my future, that I'll never make a living as an artist.

But I know what I want, and it's not what he wants for me.

Sam wondered if these entries could be relevant to the case.

Was Selena feeling trapped by her brother's overprotectiveness? Did this tension lead to her murder?

Detective Sam Taylor sat down with Daniel, his expression firm. "Daniel, I need to ask you some questions about your behavior towards Selena. Selena's notebook and diary entries suggest that you were overprotective and controlling. Did you feel like you were holding her back?"

Daniel's eyes flashed with anger. "I was just trying to help her! She was my sister, and I wanted to protect her."

Sam leaned forward. "I understand that, but did you ever feel like you were suffocating her? Did you ever resent her for not being the favored child?"

Daniel's face turned red with rage. "You think I killed her because she was the favored child? That's ridiculous!"

Sam raised an eyebrow. "I'm just asking questions, Daniel. Can you tell me where you were between 9 pm and 10 pm on the night Selena went missing?"

Daniel hesitated before speaking. "I... I was at the gym. I went for a run and then did some weights. I didn't get back until around 10:30."

Sam pulled out his notebook again. "Can anyone confirm this alibi?"

Daniel's eyes darted around the room before settling back on Sam. "I don't think so... but I'm sure it's true."

Sam sensed that Daniel was hiding something, but he didn't know what. He decided to keep pushing.

"Daniel, can you tell me more about your relationship with Selena's parents? Did they ever favor Selena over you?"

Daniel's expression turned cold. "They were always distant towards me. They never understood me or my talents. But that's not relevant to this case."

Sam detected a hint of resentment in Daniel's tone.

He made a mental note to investigate further into Daniel's relationship with his parents.

Sam checked Selena's diary for any possible reference.

Selena's Notebook

I had a fight with Mom and Dad again today.

They're so mean to Daniel, and I feel guilty for not standing up for him more.

But sometimes I just can't take it anymore.

I found out that Daniel has been going through my phone and reading my messages without me knowing.

I'm so angry and hurt. Why can't he just leave me alone?

Sam wondered if these entries could be relevant to the case.

Was Daniel's behavior towards Selena motivated by jealousy or resentment towards their parents?

Detective Sam Taylor decided to investigate Selena's parents, Lucas and Jasmine Martin.

He paid a visit to their luxurious home, trying to get a better understanding of their relationship with their children.

As he sat down in their living room, he couldn't help but notice the stark contrast between this opulent home and Selena's modest apartment.

"Can you tell me more about your relationship with your children?" Sam asked.

Lucas and Jasmine exchanged a glance before speaking in unison. "We love our children dearly, of course. But we have high expectations for them. We want them to succeed and make the most of their talents."

Sam raised an eyebrow. "High expectations can be tough on kids. Did you ever feel like you were pushing them too hard?"

Jasmine hesitated before speaking. "Perhaps... Daniel was always sensitive to criticism. Selena, on the other hand, was more resilient."

Sam sensed a subtle hint of favoritism. "And what about your relationship with Daniel? Did you ever feel like he was jealous of Selena's talents?"

Lucas's expression turned cold. "Daniel is a brilliant individual, but he's not as... artistic as Selena. We encouraged her to pursue her passion for art, while Daniel focused on his business career."

Sam pulled out his notebook again. "Can you tell me more about Selena's artistic talents? Did she ever show promise?"

Jasmine nodded enthusiastically. "Oh, yes! She was a prodigy from a young age. We thought she might make a name for herself in the art world."

Sam detected a hint of sadness in Jasmine's tone. "But it sounds like you were also disappointed when she decided to leave school and pursue art full-time?"

Lucas's face turned red with anger. "That was a foolish decision! She should have followed her parents' advice and pursued a stable career."

Sam realized that Selena's parents might have been more invested in her success than he initially thought.

Sam quickly checked Selena's diary for references.

Selena's Notebook

I had an argument with Mom and Dad again today.

They want me to give up on my art and get a 'real job'.

I feel so trapped and suffocated by their expectations.

I found an old painting by my mom when I was cleaning out the attic.

It's beautiful! I never knew she was an artist too.

Maybe I'm not the only one who has hidden talents...

Sam wondered if these entries could be relevant to the case.

Was Selena feeling trapped by her parents' expectations, or was there something more to her relationship with them?

Detective Sam Taylor decided to investigate Lucas and Jasmine's business dealings.

He learned that they owned a successful art company, Martin Arts, and were known for their ruthless business tactics.

As he delved deeper into their business records, he discovered that they had been involved in several high-stakes deals in the past few years.

There were whispers of shady dealings and conflicts with rival companies.

Sam decided to pay a visit to the Martin's office, hoping to get a better understanding of their business dealings.

He met with Lucas and Jasmine, who seemed evasive and nervous.

"Can you tell me more about your recent business dealings?" Sam asked.

Lucas and Jasmine exchanged a glance before speaking in unison. "We've had our fair share of successes and setbacks, but nothing out of the ordinary."

Sam detected a hint of unease. "I've heard rumors of conflicts with rival companies. Can you confirm or deny?"

Jasmine's expression turned cold. "We don't comment on rumors."

Sam pulled out his notebook again. "I've also heard that you've been struggling financially. Is that true?"

Lucas's face turned red with anger. "That's none of your business! We're doing just fine, thank you very much."

Sam sensed that Lucas and Jasmine were hiding something.

He made a mental note to look into their financial records further.

Sam explores Selena's diary to find any relevant clues.

Selena's Notebook

I had a fight with Mom and Dad today about my art again.

They think I'm wasting my time and that I should focus on something more practical. I feel like I'm losing myself in their expectations.

I found out that Mom and Dad have been lying to me about our financial situation.

We're actually struggling to stay afloat.

I feel so betrayed and hurt.

Sam wondered if Selena's parents' financial struggles could be related to their business dealings or if it was just a personal issue.

Detective Sam Taylor decided to investigate the Martin's financial records further.

He obtained a warrant and accessed their financial documents, only to find that they were indeed struggling financially.

The company was deeply in debt, and Lucas and Jasmine's personal finances were also suffering.

As he dug deeper, he discovered that they had been using their art business as a front for laundering money from illegal activities.

Sam was shocked by the extent of their corruption.

He realized that Selena's parents' financial struggles could be a motive for her murder, but he still needed to find a connection between their financial issues and Selena's death.

Selena's Notebook

I'm so angry with Mom and Dad right now.

They're always lying to me about our financial situation.

I feel like I'm living a lie. I wish I could tell them how I really feel, but I'm scared of what they might do.

I've been noticing some strange things around the house lately.

Mom and Dad have been arguing a lot more often, and they've been getting into fights with the neighbors.

I don't know what's going on, but I don't like it.

Sam wondered if Selena had stumbled upon something incriminating or if she was just sensing the tension in her parents' relationship.

Detective Sam Taylor decided to search Selena's room for any evidence that might link her parents' financial struggles to her murder.

He carefully went through her belongings, looking for anything out of the ordinary.

As he searched, he found a folder filled with receipts and documents related to Selena's art supplies.

It seemed that she had been buying materials in bulk, but the amounts were excessive.

Sam wondered if Selena was using her art as a way to cope with her parents' financial struggles.

He also found a series of sketches and paintings that seemed to depict Selena's feelings of isolation and desperation.

One painting in particular caught his eye - it was a dark and ominous piece that seemed to capture the feeling of being trapped.

Sam realized that Selena's art might be a key to understanding her state of mind around the time of her desertion.

He made a mental note to interview her art teacher and ask about Selena's emotional state during that period.

Selena's Notebook

I feel so alone.

Mom and Dad are always fighting, and I don't know what to do.

I feel like I'm just going through the motions, waiting for something to change.

I wish I could just disappear and leave it all behind.

I had a weird dream last night.

I was trapped in a dark room, and I couldn't find a way out.

I woke up feeling so anxious and scared.

I wish I could shake this feeling off.

Sam wondered if Selena's dream was connected to her feelings of being trapped in her parents' toxic relationship.

Detective Sam Taylor arrived at Selena's art school and asked to speak with her art teacher, Ms. Watson. She was a kind-eyed woman with a warm smile, and she welcomed Sam into her studio.

"Selena was a talented student," Ms. Watson said. "She had a unique perspective and a passion for art that was unmatched. But...there was something about her during the summer that worried me."

"What was that?" Sam asked.

"Well, Selena seemed...distracted," Ms. Watson said. "She would often forget her assignments or miss classes. And when she did come to class, she seemed distant, like she was lost in thought. I tried to talk to her about it, but she just shrugged it off and said she was fine."

Sam's eyes narrowed. "Did you notice anything else unusual?"

"Actually, yes," Ms. Watson said. "Selena started bringing in these...dark paintings. They were intense, emotional pieces that seemed to capture her inner turmoil. I asked her about them, and she just said they were 'expressing her feelings'. But...there was something about them that seemed...off."

Sam thanked Ms. Watson for her time and left the studio, his mind racing with possibilities.

Sam scanned Selena's diary for any reference.

Selena's Notebook

I've been feeling so trapped lately.

Mom and Dad are always fighting, and I feel like I'm just going through the motions.

I've been having these terrible nightmares about being buried alive.

I feel like I'm suffocating under the weight of my own life.

I found an old photo of myself when I was younger, happy and carefree.

It's like looking at a stranger.

What happened to that girl?

When did I become this person who feels so lost and alone?

Sam wondered if Selena's feelings of being trapped were connected to her parents' financial struggles or something deeper.

Detective Sam Taylor decided to pay a visit to the neighbors who had conflicts with the Martins, to see if they noticed anything suspicious on or before the time of Selena's death.

He arrived at the Hughes' house, where he was greeted by a gruff-looking man named Tom.

"Ah, you're the detective," Tom said, eyeing Sam warily. "I've been expecting you. We've been saying some things about the Martins."

"What kind of things?" Sam asked.

"Well, they've been causing quite a ruckus lately," Tom said. "Playing their music too loud, having loud arguments...it's been a real nuisance. And Selena, she was always getting into it with her parents. I saw her storming out of the house more than once, looking like she was about to lose it."

Sam's ears perked up. "Did you notice anything unusual on or before the day Selena died?"

Tom thought for a moment. "Now that you mention it, I did see something strange. I was outside working on my car when I saw Selena arguing with someone on her front porch. It was around 8 pm, and she looked really upset. I didn't think much of it at the time, but now that you mention it...maybe it was important."

Sam made a note in his pad. "Do you know who she was arguing with?"

Tom shook his head. "No, I didn't get a good look. But it was definitely someone she knew. She wasn't yelling at some stranger."

Sam thanked Tom for his information and left the Hughes' house, his mind racing with possibilities.

Selena's Notebook

I'm so sick of this fight between Mom and Dad.

They're always yelling and screaming, and I feel like I'm going crazy.

I wish they would just stop fighting and be happy for once.

I had a weird dream last night.

I was walking through a dark forest, and I saw my parents' faces on trees.

They were laughing and smiling, and it was like they were trying to lure me in.

I woke up feeling really uneasy and unsure of what's going on.

Sam wondered if Selena's argument with someone on her front porch was connected to her parents' marital issues or something deeper.

Detective Sam Taylor decided to investigate the person who was arguing with Selena on her front porch to see if they noticed anything suspicious.

He arrived at the Watson' house, where he found Selena's art teacher, Ms. Watson, sitting on the porch with a cup of tea.

"Ah, detective," she said, smiling.

"I've been expecting you. I remember that night quite clearly. It was around 8 pm, and I was working on some projects in my studio when I saw Selena arguing with someone on her front porch. I didn't recognize the person, but Selena seemed really upset."

Sam pulled out his notebook. "Can you describe the person to me?"

Ms. Watson thought for a moment. "It was a young man, maybe around Selena's age. He had messy brown hair and a scruffy beard. He was wearing a black hoodie, and he looked like he had just rolled out of bed."

Sam's eyes narrowed. "Did you see which direction he went after they argued?"

Ms. Watson shook her head. "No, I didn't see him leave. But I did notice that Selena seemed really shaken after the argument. She came back inside and went straight to her room without saying a word to anyone."

Sam thanked Ms. Watson for her information and left the Watson' house, his mind racing with possibilities.

Sam looked in Selena's dairy for any clues.

Selena's Notebook

I feel so trapped in my life right now.

I'm stuck in this small town with no prospects and no friends to speak of.

I feel like I'm just going through the motions, waiting for something to happen.

I had a dream last night that I was flying.

It felt so real, like I was actually soaring above the trees and feeling free.

But when I woke up, it was like it never happened at all.

Sam wondered if Selena's argument with the young man on her front porch was connected to her feelings of being trapped or her desire for something else.

Detective Sam Taylor decided to investigate local teenagers with messy brown hair and beards to see if any of them match the description.

After canvassing the local high school and nearby art schools, he finally got a lead on a 26-year-old artist named Owen who matched the description.

Sam checked his notes and found that Owen was already on his suspect list for investigation.

Detective Sam Taylor sat in his office, going over the case files and notes.

He couldn't shake the feeling that he was missing something.

He decided to pay a visit to Owen, the artist Selena had met at the exhibit.

As he arrived at Owen's studio, he was struck by the vibrant colors and eclectic decor.

Owen himself answered the door, looking every bit the charming artist.

"Hey, detective! Come on in," he said, ushering Sam into the studio.

Sam took out his notebook. "Owen, I need to ask you some questions about your relationship with Selena. Can you tell me about your last interaction with her?"

Owen's expression turned thoughtful. "We had dinner together a few nights ago. She was really struggling with her art, feeling stuck and uncertain about her future. I tried to offer some encouragement and advice."

Sam sensed that there was more to the story. "Did you notice anything unusual about her behavior that night?"

Owen hesitated before speaking. "She seemed... anxious. Like she was hiding something from me."

Sam's ears perked up at this new information. "Do you know what she might have been hiding?"

Owen shrugged. "No idea. But I do remember she mentioned something about getting a new commission from a wealthy client."

Sam made a mental note to look into this new lead.

As he left Owen's studio, Sam couldn't help but feel that he was supportive here. He decided to investigate further into Selena's art world connections.

Detective Sam Taylor sat in front of his computer, scrolling through Selena's social media accounts once again.

He had already found some suspicious messages and comments, but he wanted to dig deeper.

As he scrolled through her Instagram posts, he noticed a pattern.

Selena often posted about her art, sharing sketches and paintings with her followers.

But there was one post that caught his eye - a drawing of a figure with a red X marked through it.

Sam's mind racing, he decided to investigate further.

He searched for any mentions of the same symbol online, hoping to find a connection to Selena's murder.

After some digging, he found a Reddit thread discussing the same symbol.

It was an old meme from a few years ago, but one commenter mentioned using it to symbolize "fake art" or "sell-outs".

Sam's eyes widened as he realized that this might be a lead. He decided to pay a visit to Selena's art school and talk to her former classmates.

Maybe someone had seen her using the symbol or knew something about her feelings towards other artists.

As he arrived at the art school, he was greeted by the familiar scent of paint and turpentine. He approached one of the teachers, an older woman with kind eyes.

"Hi, I'm Detective Taylor. I'm investigating the death of Selena Martin, one of your former students. Can you tell me more about her time here?"

The teacher nodded thoughtfully. "Selena was a talented student, but she struggled with self-doubt and competition. She often felt like she didn't fit in with the other students."

Sam's ears perked up at this new information. "Did she ever mention any specific rivalries or conflicts?"

The teacher hesitated before speaking. "Well... there was one student who seemed particularly upset with Selena. His name is Austin, and they had a disagreement about their art styles."

Sam made a mental note to look into Austin's alibi and see if he had any connection to Selena's murder.

Detective Sam Taylor arrived at Austin's studio, eager to question him about his possible connection to Selena's murder.

As he entered the studio, he was struck by the stark contrast between Austin's work and Selena's. Austin's paintings were bold and vibrant, while Selena's had been more subtle and introspective.

Austin himself answered the door, looking like a deer caught in the headlights. "Can I help you?" he asked nervously.

Sam flashed his badge. "I'm Detective Taylor. I'm investigating Selena Martin's murder.

I understand you had a disagreement with her about art?"

Austin nodded sheepishly. "Yeah, we had some differences of opinion. But I didn't kill her!"

Sam pulled out his notebook. "Can you tell me more about your argument? When did it happen?"

Austin sighed. "It was at an art show a few months ago. We both had pieces on display, and we argued about whose work was better."

Sam's eyes narrowed. "Did it get physical?"

Austin shook his head. "No, no, nothing like that. We just... got loud. And then we parted ways."

Sam thanked Austin for his time and left the studio, thinking about the alibi Austin had provided.

As he walked back to his car, he couldn't shake the feeling that something wasn't quite right.

He decided to look into Austin's social media accounts and see if he had posted anything suspicious around the time of the argument.

Back at the station, Sam spent hours digging through Austin's online presence.

Finally, he found a post from around the time of the argument - a cryptic message that read: "Some people will stop at nothing to get ahead".

Sam's eyes widened as he realized this might be a red flag.

Detective Sam Taylor walked back to Austin's studio, determined to get to the bottom of the cryptic post.

When he arrived, Austin was sitting at his easel, painting a vibrant landscape.

"Austin, I need to ask you some more questions," Sam said, his tone firm but calm.

Austin looked up, concerned. "What's going on?"

Sam pulled out his phone and showed Austin the post. "This was on your social media account around the time of the argument with Selena. What does it mean?"

Austin's eyes widened in surprise. "Oh, that? I don't know what you're talking about."

Sam's gut told him that Austin was lying. "Don't play dumb, Austin. You know exactly what I'm talking about. What did you mean by 'some people will stop at nothing to get ahead'?"

Austin sighed and rubbed his temples. "Fine. I said that in a moment of anger. I didn't mean anything by it."

Sam leaned forward. "What did you mean by it? Was Selena one of those people?"

Austin hesitated before speaking. "Selena and I had... differences. She thought my art was shallow, that I was just trying to make a quick buck. And I thought she was too pretentious, too focused on her own ego."

Sam's eyes narrowed. "And did this argument escalate to physical violence?"

Austin shook his head. "No, no, nothing like that. Like I said, we usually... get loud. And later we part our ways."

Sam thanked Austin for his explanation and left the studio, but felt suspicious.

As he walked back to his car, he couldn't help but wonder what other secrets Austin might be hiding.

Detective Sam Taylor sat at his desk, scrolling through Selena's social media accounts.

He found a post from around the time Austin's cryptic message, but it was innocuous - a photo of her latest art piece with a caption about the inspiration behind it.

He continued to dig through her online presence, searching for any hints of threats or animosity towards Austin or anyone else.

Finally, he found a private message thread between Selena and an unknown user.

The conversation started with an innocuous comment about Selena's art, but soon turned dark. The user, who identified themselves only as "Observer", made several threatening comments about Selena's work and her perceived arrogance.

Sam's eyes narrowed as he read through the exchange.

This could be the break they needed to crack the case.

As he continued to read, he noticed that the messages stopped abruptly around the time of Selena's murder.

He wondered if Observer was somehow connected to Selena's death.

Detective Sam Taylor walked back to Austin's studio, determined to share the new evidence with him.

As he entered the studio, he saw Austin working on a new piece, his brow furrowed in concentration.

"Austin, I need to show you something," Sam said, pulling out his phone.

Austin looked up; his eyes curious. "What is it?"

Sam showed him the private message thread between Selena and Observer.

Austin's expression changed from curiosity to alarm.

"Where did you find these?" he asked, his voice shaking slightly.

Sam leaned forward. "They were in Selena's social media account. Does this look familiar to you?"

Austin's eyes scanned the screen, his face pale. "I... I don't recognize the tone or style. But I do remember something similar from our argument."

Sam's eyes narrowed. "What did you mean by 'similar'?"

Austin hesitated before speaking. "Selena would often say things that were... biting, cutting. She would make fun of my work, call me shallow. I thought it was just her being Selena, but maybe it was more than that."

Sam's mind was racing. This new information raised more questions than answers.

Was Austin hiding something? Was Selena's behavior more sinister than they thought?

As they continued to discuss the messages, Sam noticed a notebook lying open on Austin's worktable.

The pages were filled with sketches of people, their faces twisted in anger or sadness.

"Austin, what's this?" Sam asked, pointing to the notebook.

Austin's eyes dropped. "Just some ideas for a new piece. I was experimenting with different emotions."

Sam's gut told him that there was more to it than that. He made a mental note to ask Austin more about the notebook later.

Detective Sam Taylor decided to expand the investigation to look for other potential suspects who might have had a motive to kill Selena.

He started by visiting her acquaintances and colleagues, asking if they noticed anything unusual or suspicious about her behavior in the days leading up to her death.

One person who caught his attention was a woman named Amy, who had been a close friend of Selena's since college.

Amy seemed nervous and fidgety during their conversation, but Sam couldn't quite put his finger on what it was.

"What do you think might have motivated someone to kill Selena?" Sam asked, leaning forward.

Amy hesitated before speaking. "I don't know... but I did notice that Selena was getting more and more withdrawn lately. She would cancel plans at the last minute, and when we did hang out, she seemed distant and preoccupied."

Sam's eyes narrowed. This could be a lead worth exploring further.

As he left Amy's apartment, he couldn't help but think about Selena's diary entries.

He had found them scattered throughout her studio, each one detailing her struggles with anxiety and depression.

He wondered if these struggles might have been related to her murder.

Back at the station, Sam decided to dig deeper into Selena's past, looking for any potential connections between her mental health and her death.

He discovered that Selena had been struggling with anxiety and depression for years, and had even been hospitalized briefly after a particularly severe episode.

This new information raised more questions than answers.

Had Selena's mental health struggles driven someone to kill her? Or was there something more sinister at play?

Detective Sam Taylor decided to investigate Amy further, to see if she noticed anything else unusual about Selena's behavior.

He arrived at Amy's apartment, and she greeted him with a nervous smile.

"So, Amy, you mentioned that Selena was getting more and more withdrawn in the days leading up to her death. Did you notice anything specific that might be related to her murder?" Sam asked.

Amy hesitated, glancing around the room as if ensuring they were alone. "Well, I did notice that Selena was getting into some kind of argument with someone online. I saw her typing furiously on her laptop, and then she stormed out of here. I didn't think much of it at the time, but maybe it's relevant?"

Sam's ears perked up. This was a new lead. "Can you show me what you saw?"

Amy nodded and pulled out her phone. "I took a screenshot of her laptop screen. It was a chat log with someone named 'Observer'. The conversation seemed really intense."

Sam's eyes scanned the chat log. It was a heated exchange, with both Selena and Observer using aggressive language.

"Did you recognize this person?" Sam asked Amy.

Amy shook her head. "No, I don't think so. But Selena mentioned something about meeting this person in person recently. She seemed really upset about it."

Sam made a mental note to look into Observer's identity and connection to Selena.

He also wondered if this online argument might have been a red herring or a genuine motive for the murder.

As he left Amy's apartment, Sam couldn't help but think about Selena's notebook entries again. One particular passage caught his eye:

Selena's Notebook

I feel like I'm living in a prison of my own making.

Every day is a struggle to keep my anxiety at bay, and I'm exhausted from pretending to be someone I'm not.

I just want to break free and be myself, but what if no one likes the real me?

Sam felt a pang of sadness for Selena.

He realized that she might have been struggling with feelings of inadequacy and self-doubt, which could have contributed to her isolation and vulnerability.

Detective Sam Taylor decided to investigate Observer's identity and connection to Selena.

He started by searching online for any matches, but the username was too generic to yield any concrete results.

Detective Sam Taylor sat in front of his computer, determined to track down the IP address of the mysterious user, Observer.

He poured over the private message thread, searching for any clues that might lead him to the culprit.

As he worked, he found himself wondering about Selena's life beyond her art.

What had driven her to create such powerful pieces?

What had made her so confident and yet so vulnerable?

Sam couldn't help but feel a pang of empathy for Selena.

He knew what it was like to feel like you weren't being taken seriously.

He refocused on the task at hand, determined to track down Observer.

He spent hours tracing the digital trail, finally managing to isolate the location of the original message.

It was a small internet cafe in a rundown part of town.

Sam decided to pay a visit to the cafe, hoping to get more information.

As he walked in, he was hit with the smell of stale coffee and worn-out keyboards.

The staff was friendly, but reluctant to talk about their customers.

Sam flashed his badge and asked if anyone remembered Selena Martin visiting the cafe.

One of the employees, a young woman with a purple streak in her hair, spoke up.

"Yeah, we saw her a few times. She'd come in late at night, usually around 2 or 3 am. She'd sit alone at a table in the back, typing away on her laptop."

Sam's eyes narrowed. "Do you remember what she was working on?"

The employee hesitated before speaking. "It looked like she was writing something... intense. She'd scribble notes all over her paper, and sometimes she'd rip them out and crumple them up."

Sam thanked the employee and left the cafe, feeling like he was getting closer to the truth.

Back at his office, he pulled out Selena's notebook and began to flip through the pages.

As he reached a certain entry, his eyes widened.

The entry was dated two nights ago - around the same time Selena was seen at the internet cafe.

Selena's Notebook

I can't believe what I've found out about Austin.

He's been lying to me this whole time.

He's not just some struggling artist; he's been playing me from the start.

I feel like I've been blinded by my own ego.

I need to get out of this toxic situation before it's too late.

Sam's eyes scanned the page, searching for any other clues. That's when he saw it - a small note in the margin.

Meet me at Old Town Park at midnight.

Sam's gut told him that this was where Selena had planned to meet someone on that fateful night.

Detective Sam Taylor decided to confront Austin about Selena's accusations.

He arrived at Austin's studio, his heart racing with anticipation.

Austin answered the door, looking worried. "What's going on, Sam?"

Sam took a deep breath. "I need to ask you some questions about Selena. Specifically, about her accusations that you've been lying to her."

Austin's expression changed from worry to defensiveness. "What are you talking about? I told you; we were just friends."

Sam pulled out Selena's notebook and showed him the entry. "This says otherwise. You've been playing her, using her for your own gain."

Austin's eyes dropped. "I... I didn't mean to hurt her. I was just trying to get ahead in my career."

Sam's eyes narrowed. "Get ahead how? By manipulating Selena?"

Austin hesitated before speaking. "Maybe I did take advantage of her attention. But she was always willing to help me out, and I thought we were... close."

Sam felt a surge of anger. "Close? You call using someone like that 'close'?"

Austin sighed. "Look, Sam, I know I made a mistake. But I never meant for it to end like this."

Sam's mind was racing.

This seemed like a motive for murder, but something didn't add up.

As they continued to talk, Sam noticed a small photograph on Austin's desk.

It was a picture of Selena and Austin together, smiling and happy.

"What's this?" Sam asked.

Austin's eyes clouded over. "That was just one night, Sam. A mistake on my part."

Sam's gut told him that there was more to the story.

Detective Sam Taylor decided to press Austin for more information about the photograph. "What's the story behind this?" he asked, holding up the picture.

Austin sighed, looking away. "It was just one night, Sam. I was going through a tough time, and Selena was... comforting me. We had a moment, okay? It meant nothing."

Sam's eyes narrowed. "Nothing?"

Austin hesitated before speaking. "We had a connection, yeah. But it was casual. We both knew it was a mistake."

Sam's mind was racing. He didn't believe Austin's story. "What did Selena say to you that night?"

Austin's eyes dropped. "She told me she loved me."

Sam felt a pang of sadness for Selena.

She had given her heart to someone who didn't deserve it.

As they continued to talk, Sam noticed that Austin seemed nervous, glancing around the room as if he was worried someone was listening.

"Austin, what are you hiding?" Sam asked.

Austin sighed, rubbing his temples. "I don't know what you're talking about."

Sam pulled out Selena's notebook and flipped through the pages, stopping at an entry dated a few weeks ago.

Selena's Notebook

I had the most incredible night with Austin.

We talked about our dreams and aspirations, and for once,
I felt like I was really seen.

He's charming and talented, but there's something about him that makes me feel like I'm walking on eggshells.

Sam looked up at Austin. "You're hiding something, Austin. I can see it in your eyes."

Austin's eyes flashed with anger before he regained control. "I'm hiding nothing, Sam."

Sam's gut told him that Austin was lying again.

Detective Sam Taylor decided to confront Austin about the inconsistency in his story. "Austin, I've been going over Selena's notebook, and I noticed that you told me you and Selena were just friends. But here, in her own words, she writes about having a special connection with you. Which one is true?"

Austin's eyes darted around the room before he looked back at Sam. "I... I was just trying to protect her feelings. We didn't mean anything by it."

Sam's eyes narrowed. "Protect her feelings? By lying to me and everyone else about your relationship?"

Austin sighed, rubbing his temples. "Look, Sam, I know I wasn't honest with you, but it's because I didn't want anyone to know about our little secret. Selena was... fragile. She needed someone to lean on, and I took advantage of that."

Sam's gut told him that Austin was hiding something more sinister than just a harmless crush.

Sam looked in Selena's dairy for more clues.

Selena's Notebook

I found out that Austin has been lying to me.

He told me we were just friends, but his eyes told a different story.

I feel like I'm stuck in a nightmare, unsure of what to do.

I had a fight with my best friend, June.

We've been drifting apart for months, but this was the final straw.

She says I'm too consumed by Austin and that I'm not the same person anymore.

Maybe she's right.

Sam's mind racing, he wondered if June might be more involved in Selena's death than he initially thought.

Detective Sam Taylor decided to ask Austin about his alibi on the night of Selena's death. "Austin, can you tell me where you were between 10pm and 1am on the night of Selena's death?"

Austin hesitated before speaking. "I was... out with some friends. We went to a movie and then grabbed some late-night coffee."

Sam's eyes narrowed. "Which friends? And can they corroborate your alibi?"

Austin's expression turned defensive. "I don't see why that's relevant. I'm just telling you what happened."

Sam's gut told him that Austin was hiding something, but he needed concrete evidence to prove it. Sam looked in Selena's diary for more connections.

Selena's Notebook

I've been feeling trapped in this studio, surrounded by Austin's charm and charisma.

But when we're alone, he's distant and cold.

I feel like I'm just a pawn in his game.

I got a call from my mom today.

She's been trying to get me to come home, but I don't want to go back to that toxic environment.

I feel like I'm running away from my problems, but I need space to figure out who I am without the pressure of everyone else's expectations.

Sam wondered if Selena's troubled past was connected to her death. But first he needs to search Austin's studio for any leads.

Detective Sam Taylor decided to search Austin's studio for any physical evidence but he knows that he would need a search warrant to do an official search.

Sam quickly headed back and came next day.

He obtained a warrant and began searching the space, looking for anything that might be connected to Selena's death.

As he searched, he found a small, hidden compartment in Austin's desk drawer. Inside, he found a letter addressed to Selena.

Sam's eyes narrowed as he read the letter.

It seemed to suggest that Austin was aware of Selena's vulnerabilities and was using that knowledge to manipulate her.

Sam thought of checking Selena's dairy of any further leads.

Letter Undated

Austin,

I know I've been distant lately, but it's because I'm trying to protect you from the truth.

I've been watching you, and I know you're not as strong as you think you are.

You're vulnerable, and I'm not sure you can handle the truth.

Selena's Notebook

I had a strange dream last night.

I was back in my childhood home, surrounded by the same familiar walls and furniture.

But this time, I was alone.

No one was there to comfort me or tell me everything would be okay. I woke up feeling lost and scared.

Detective Sam Taylor couldn't find any comparison with the letter in her notebook diary.

He decided to confront Austin about the letter and its contents, and asked him to explain.

Austin's expression turned cold. "I don't know what you're talking about."

Sam's eyes narrowed. "Don't lie to me, Austin. This letter suggests you knew Selena's vulnerabilities and were trying to manipulate her. What's going on?"

Austin's expression turned defiant. "You're just trying to pin this on me because you can't solve it otherwise."

Sam's gut told him that Austin was hiding something, but he needed concrete evidence to prove it.

Sam returned to his office and thought how he can get Austin to spill the truth.

Suddenly he remembered about the small note he found in the margin which says, "Meet me at Old Town Park at midnight".

Sam wondered if he could find some clue there. He decided to go to Old Town Park and investigate.

Detective Sam Taylor arrived at Old Town Park just before midnight, the moon casting an eerie glow over the deserted landscape.

He had a flashlight in hand, his eyes scanning the area for any sign of activity.

As he walked through the park, he noticed a figure sitting on a bench, huddled in a coat.

Sam approached cautiously, his hand on his gun.

The figure looked up, startled.

It was a young woman, probably in her early twenties, with a look of exhaustion on her face.

"Can I help you?" she asked, her voice trembling.

Sam flashed his badge. "I'm Detective Taylor. I'm investigating the death of Selena Martin. Can you tell me what you're doing here?"

The woman hesitated before speaking. "I... I was supposed to meet someone here tonight. Selena and I were supposed to meet."

Sam's eyes narrowed. "Selena? As in, Selena Martin?"

The woman nodded. "Yes. We were supposed to meet at midnight to discuss something important."

Sam's mind raced. Was this woman a witness or a suspect? He decided to play it cool.

"Can you tell me more about what you know?" he asked, pulling out his notebook.

The woman took a deep breath before speaking. "Selena and I have been friends for a while now. We met online, through an art community forum. We'd talk about our passion for art and share our work with each other."

Sam's ears perked up at this new information. "An art community forum? Do you remember the name of the forum?"

The woman thought for a moment before speaking. "I think it was... Artistic Hub?"

Sam's eyes lit up. This was the name he saw on Selena's online activities.

Detective Sam Taylor sat down next to the woman on the bench, his eyes locked on hers. "Can you tell me more about what you and Selena were going to discuss tonight?" he asked.

The woman hesitated before speaking. "We were going to meet up and talk about a project we're working on together. We're both artists, and we've been collaborating on a graphic novel."

Sam's ears perked up. "A graphic novel? What's the story about?"

The woman's eyes darted around the park before settling back on Sam. "It's... it's a bit complicated. Let's just say it's a personal project for us."

Sam sensed that she was holding back, but he didn't press the issue.

Instead, he decided to ask more questions about their relationship.

"What was Selena like as a person?" he asked.

The woman's expression turned somber. "Selena was an amazing person. She was talented, kind, and passionate about her art. We became close friends over the past year, bonding over our shared love of art and music."

Sam noticed that she seemed genuinely grief-stricken by Selena's death.

"Did you notice anything unusual about Selena in the days leading up to her death?" he asked.

The woman thought for a moment before speaking. "Actually, yes. She seemed... anxious. Like something was weighing on her mind. But she wouldn't talk about it."

Sam's instincts told him that this was important information. He made a mental note to look into Selena's online activities around that time.

As they finished their conversation, Sam thanked the woman for her time and promised to keep her safe.

As he walked away from the bench, he pulled out Selena's notebook and flipped through the pages once more.

Selena's Notebook

I'm so torn about this project.

Austin is pushing me to make changes I don't believe in, but if I don't comply, he threatens to ruin my reputation.

I feel trapped.

Sam's eyes widened as he realized that Selena had been struggling with Austin, just as the woman had said.

Detective Sam Taylor walked back to the station, his mind racing with the new information he had gathered.

He decided to review the case files and see if he could find any connections between Selena's death and her personal life.

As he sat down at his desk, he pulled out the case files and began to read through them again.

He noticed that Selena had been a successful artist, with a promising career ahead of her.

She had no known enemies, and her family and friends all seemed to be genuinely grieving her loss.

Sam flipped through the pages, looking for any inconsistencies or red flags.

He came across a statement from Austin, Selena's boyfriend, who had said that they had a fight the night before her death.

Sam's eyes narrowed as he wondered if this fight was more significant than Austin had let on.

As he continued to review the case files, Sam noticed that Selena had received several strange emails and messages in the days leading up to her death.

They were all from unknown senders, and they seemed to be trying to intimidate or threaten Selena.

Sam's eyes scanned the emails quickly, his mind racing with possibilities. One of the emails caught his eye:

From: anonymous

You're playing with fire, Selena. You think you're so smart, but you're just a pawn in a game you don't understand. Stop playing along or face the consequences.

Sam's gut told him that this email was connected to Selena's murder. He made a mental note to investigate further.

Detective Sam Taylor decided to investigate the unknown senders of the emails.

He started by analyzing the emails themselves, looking for any clues that might lead him to the sender. One email caught his eye:

From: anonymous

You're so close, Selena. But you'll never be free.

Sam noticed that the email was sent from a public internet café, but the IP address was masked.

He made a note to investigate the café and see if anyone remembered Selena visiting around the time the email was sent.

As he dug deeper, Sam found another email:

From: anonymous

You're playing with fire, Selena. You'll burn for your mistakes.

Sam realized that these emails were not just random threats, but seemed to be connected to Selena's art project.

He made a mental note to look into her art projects and see if she had been working on something sensitive.

As he continued to investigate, Sam came across a passage in Selena's notebook:

Selena's Notebook

I'm so scared.

I think I've made a mistake.

I didn't mean to hurt anyone, but now it's too late.

I don't know what to do.

Sam's eyes widened as he read the passage.

It seemed that Selena had been struggling with her conscience, possibly about something related to her art project.

Detective Sam Taylor decided to investigate Selena's art project, hoping to find a connection to the threatening emails.

He arrived at Selena's studio, a small but cozy space filled with art supplies and half-finished canvases.

As he began to look through her work, Sam noticed a series of paintings that seemed to depict a young woman, possibly Selena herself, surrounded by flames.

The paintings were eerie and unsettling, and Sam couldn't help but wonder what they meant.

He also found a collection of newspaper clippings and articles about a local protest movement that had been gaining momentum in the weeks leading up to Selena's death.

The movement was focused on exposing the truth about a local business owner who had been accused of shady dealings.

Sam's eyes widened as he realized that Selena's art project might be connected to the protest movement.

He made a mental note to investigate the business owner and see if there was any connection to Selena's death.

Sam checked Selena's diary of any connection:

Selena's Notebook

I'm so torn. I feel like I'm being pulled in two directions.

On one hand, I want to expose the truth about the Collins' business dealings. They're hurting so many people, and someone needs to stand up for them.

But on the other hand, I'm scared.

I know they have powerful connections and could ruin my career if they find out what I'm working on.

Sam realized that Selena had been struggling with her own moral dilemma, caught between her desire to do what was right and her fear of the consequences.

Detective Sam Taylor decided to investigate the Collins' business dealings, hoping to find a connection to Selena's death.

He arrived at the Collins's office building, a modern structure that seemed out of place in the otherwise quiet neighborhood.

As he began to ask questions, Sam learned that the Collins were a prominent family in the community, known for their charitable donations and philanthropic efforts.

However, rumors had been circulating about their questionable business practices, including allegations of embezzlement and fraud.

Sam's eyes narrowed as he listened to the allegations.

It seemed that Selena had been digging deep into the Collins' business dealings, and her art project might have been a way to expose their wrongdoings.

As he continued to investigate, Sam came across a passage in Selena's notebook:

Selena's Notebook

I finally got access to their financial records.

It's like I knew it would be.

They're hiding something big, and I'm going to uncover it.

But I'm scared. What if they find out?

Sam realized that Selena had been getting close to uncovering something significant, but she was also terrified of the consequences.

But is this related to Collins' financial records? He needs to look for more clues.

Detective Sam Taylor decided to investigate Selena's relationships with her friends and acquaintances, hoping to find someone who might have known about her involvement in the protest movement.

He thought to re-visit her friend, June whom he met earlier in the investigation.

Sam arrived at the apartment and found June sitting on the couch, staring blankly at a TV show.

She looked up as Sam introduced himself.

"I'm Detective Taylor, remember. I'm investigating Selena's death. Can I talk to you for a bit?"

June nodded, still looking somber. "Of course. I'm just...still trying to process everything."

Sam pulled out his notebook and began to ask questions. "Can you tell me about your relationship with Selena? How close were you two?"

June thought for a moment before answering. "We were pretty close. We met in art school and became fast friends. We lived together for a few years before Selena got accepted into the art program at the university."

Sam's eyes widened as he scribbled some notes. "Did Selena ever talk to you about any of her art projects or research she was working on?"

June hesitated before speaking. "Yeah, she did mention something about an art project she was working on, but she didn't go into details. She said it was going to be big, but that's all she would say."

Sam's mind was racing as he tried to connect the dots. "And did she ever mention anything about the Collins or their business dealings?"

June shook her head. "No, nothing like that. But she was really upset one day, saying that someone had been threatening her and trying to silence her. I didn't know what it was about, but I could tell she was scared."

Sam's eyes narrowed as he made a mental note to look into the threats Selena had received.

As he continued to talk to June, Sam noticed a sketchbook lying on the coffee table.

It was filled with drawings of people, places, and symbols that looked like...flowers?

"What's this?" Sam asked, picking up the sketchbook.

June smiled wistfully. "Oh, those are just some ideas Selena was working on for her art project. She loved flowers and wanted to incorporate them into her work."

Sam's mind was racing as he turned the pages, trying to see if there were any connections between the drawings and Selena's death.

Detective Sam Taylor decided to ask June more questions about Selena's research and art project.

He wanted to get a better understanding of what Selena was working on and if it was connected to her death.

"So, June, can you tell me more about Selena's art project?" Sam asked, flipping through the sketchbook.

June leaned back on the couch, thinking for a moment. "Well, she was really passionate about it. She wanted to create a series of murals that would raise awareness about social justice issues. She was particularly interested in exposing corporate corruption and inequality."

Sam's eyes lit up as he scribbled some notes. "And did she have any specific corporations in mind?"

June nodded. "Yeah, she was really focused on the Collins' company. She thought they were involved in some shady dealings and wanted to shine a light on it."

Sam's gut told him that this was a crucial lead. "Did Selena share any specific information with you about her research?"

June hesitated before speaking. "Well, she mentioned that she found some documents that suggested the Collins were involved in some kind of money laundering scheme. But she didn't go into details."

Sam's mind was racing as he tried to piece together the puzzle.

He made a mental note to look into the Collins' business dealings again, this time focusing on money laundering.

June mentioned that she will help in the investigation and will inform Sam for any leads.

Sam thanked her for the support and cooperation.

Sam requested June to call him immediately or visit his office if she finds any leads (just in case if he is not reachable).

As he continued to chat with June, Sam searched Selena's dairy and found some notes:

Selena's Notebook

I'm so close! I can feel it! I just need to find the right proof...

I've got it! I found a document that implicates them in a massive fraud scheme!

I'm going to expose them! I'll show them what it means to mess with me!

Sam's eyes widened as he read the notes. It seemed like Selena had been getting close to uncovering something big before her death.

Detective Sam Taylor decided to go back to the police station and review the case files again, looking for any other connections.

He sat down at his desk and began to sift through the documents, his mind racing with new information.

As he flipped through the files, he came across a report from Selena's phone records.

It seemed that she had made several calls to a mysterious number on the night of her death. Sam's eyes narrowed as he tried to identify the number.

Just then, June walked into the station, looking concerned. "Hey, Detective. I wanted you to see this."

Sam looked up from his files. "What is it?"

June hesitated before speaking. "I was going through Selena's belongings and I found a letter she wrote to me but I just saw it few mins back and thought to share with you. It's dated a few days before her death."

Sam's interest piqued; he asked June to hand over the letter.

As he read the letter, Sam learned more about Selena's backstory and her motivations for getting involved in the protest movement.

Letter from Selena to June

Dear June,

I've been feeling so overwhelmed lately. I know I've been distant, but it's because I've been dealing with some personal demons.

My parents were really hard on me growing up, always pushing me to be perfect. I felt like I couldn't ever make them proud.

But then I discovered my passion for art and activism. It was like I finally found a way to express myself and make a difference.

But it's hard, June. It's hard to fight against the system when it seems like everyone is against you.

I know I've been taking risks, but I feel like it's necessary. I have to speak out against injustice, even if it means putting myself in danger. Please don't worry about me, June. I'll be okay.

Love,
Selena

Sam felt a pang of sadness as he finished reading the letter.

He realized that Selena was more than just a victim - she was a complex person with her own struggles and motivations.

Detective Sam Taylor decided to follow up on the mysterious phone number Selena had called on the night of her death.

He printed out the number and began to trace it back to its owner.

After a few hours of digging, Sam finally got a hit on the number.

It belonged to a man named Liam, a freelance journalist who had been working on a story about corporate corruption.

Sam arrived at Liam's office, next to a small coffee shop in the heart of the city.

He introduced himself and requested to ask Liam a few questions.

Liam looked up from his laptop, his eyes narrowing. "What's this about?"

Sam flashed his badge. "I'm investigating the murder of Selena Martin. I understand she called you on the night of her death."

Liam's expression changed from curious to guarded. "Yeah, I remember the call. We talked about her research and art project. She was really passionate about it."

Sam's eyes locked onto Liam's. "And did she share anything specific with you about her research?"

Liam hesitated before speaking. "She mentioned something about finding a document that implicated the Collins in some kind of fraud scheme. But she didn't go into details."

Sam's mind was racing as he tried to piece together the puzzle.

He made a mental note to look into Liam's alibi for the night of Selena's death.

As he left Liam's office, Sam couldn't shake off the feeling that there was more to Selena's story than met the eye.

Detective Sam Taylor decided to investigate Selena's research further, looking for any connections to the Collins or Liam.

He headed back to the police station and began to dig through Selena's notebook and diary entries.

As he flipped through the pages, he found a note that caught his eye:

Selena's Notebook

I'm getting close to uncovering the truth.

I have a lead on a document that could expose the Collins' corrupt practices.

I'm meeting Liam tonight to discuss it further.

Sam's eyes scanned the page, taking in the urgency in Selena's writing. He made a mental note to speak with Liam again and ask about their meeting.

Next, he came across a newspaper clipping:

Newspaper Clipping

Local Businessman Accused of Embezzlement: Alan Collins, CEO of Collins Inc., has been accused of embezzling millions from his company. The investigation is ongoing.

Sam's eyes widened as he realized the potential connection between Selena's research and the Collins.

He made another note to look into Alan Collins's alibi for the night of Selena's death.

As he continued to read through Selena's notes, Sam discovered more leads and potential connections.

He realized that Selena had been working on a larger-than-life art project, using her research to expose corporate corruption.

Detective Sam Taylor decided to investigate Liam further, looking for any potential motives or connections.

He headed back to the police station and pulled up Liam's phone records.

As he scrolled through the calls and texts, he noticed a conversation with an unknown number on the night of Selena's death.

The conversation was brief, but it seemed intense. Sam's eyes narrowed as he made a mental note to track down the unknown number.

He also noticed that Liam had received a package from Selena a few days before her death, containing a USB drive and a note that read: "For your eyes only."

Sam decided to pay Liam another visit, this time with a warrant to search his office and computer.

As he arrived at Liam's office, Sam was greeted by Liam himself, looking nervous and agitated.

"Can I help you, Detective?" Liam asked, his voice shaking slightly.

Sam flashed his badge. "I'm investigating the murder of Selena Martin. I'd like to ask you some questions and take a look at your office."

Liam hesitated before nodding and leading Sam to his office. As they walked in, Sam noticed a large whiteboard covered in notes and diagrams.

"What's all this?" Sam asked, his eyes scanning the board.

"Ah, just some research for my next story," Liam replied hastily.

Sam raised an eyebrow. "Your next story?"

Liam nodded. "Yeah, I'm working on an exposé about corporate corruption. I've been gathering evidence and interviewing sources."

Sam's eyes locked onto Liam's. "And did you share any of this information with Selena?"

Liam hesitated before speaking. "We discussed some of my research, but I didn't share anything specific with her."

Sam's gut told him that Liam was hiding something. He decided to push further.

"And what about this package she sent you?" Sam asked, his eyes narrowing.

Liam looked taken aback. "Oh, that? It was just some data she wanted me to analyze. Nothing important."

Sam wasn't convinced.

Detective Sam Taylor decided to analyze the data on the USB drive and computer, which was in connection with an art and fraud scheme.

He spent hours poring over the files, trying to make sense of the complex collection of documents and emails.

As he scrolled through the files, he noticed that Selena had been investigating a large-scale art fraud scheme involving several high-end galleries and auction houses.

She had been digging deep, gathering evidence and tracking down leads.

Sam's eyes widened as he realized the scope of the scheme.

It seemed that several prominent art dealers had been collaborating to create fake art pieces, then selling them to unsuspecting collectors for exorbitant prices.

He also found a series of emails between Selena and an anonymous source, who claimed to have inside information on the scheme.

The emails were cryptic, but Sam sensed that Selena was getting close to uncovering the truth.

As he delved deeper into the files, he discovered a folder labeled "The Masterpiece".

Inside, he found a detailed plan for a massive art piece, valued at millions.

The plan was unsigned, but Sam suspected that it was Selena's work.

He also found a note from Selena, dated the day before her death:

Almost there... I can feel it. But I'm scared. They'll stop at nothing to keep their secrets safe.

Sam's gut told him that Selena would have been in grave danger.

He decided to investigate further, tracing the IP addresses and email trails to see if they led to any suspects.

Detective Sam Taylor decided to look into the background of the companies involved in the scheme, hoping to find a lead.

He started by researching the owners and executives of the companies, trying to find any connections between them.

As he delved deeper, he discovered that several of the company executives had a history of shady dealings and were known to be ruthless in their business practices.

He also found that one of the companies, a large art conservancy, Martin Arts, was run by none other than Lucas Martin, Selena's father.

Sam's eyes widened as he made the connection. Could Lucas be involved in his daughter's murder?

He decided to pay Lucas a visit, trying to keep an open mind about his intentions.

As he arrived at Lucas's office, he was greeted by a father.

"Can I help you, Detective?" Lucas asked gruffly.

Sam flashed his badge. "I hope you remember me in investigating the murder of your daughter, Selena. I understand she was working on an art fraud case?"

Lucas's expression changed from stern to calculating. "Ah, yes. Selena was always getting herself involved in things she didn't understand. I warned her about getting too close to those people."

Sam sensed that Lucas was hiding something. "What do you know about the companies involved in the scheme?"

Lucas snorted. "Those people are scoundrels. I wouldn't be surprised if they were involved in Selena's murder."

Sam's gut told him that Lucas was not telling him everything.

He decided to push further.
"And what about your own involvement with these companies?" Sam asked.

Lucas's expression turned cold. "I have business interests with some of them, yes. But I assure you, I had nothing to do with Selena's murder."

Sam wasn't convinced.

He decided to dig deeper into Lucas's background, looking for any connections to the art world or potential motives.

Detective Sam Taylor decided to investigate Lucas Martin's business dealings and potential connections to the art world.

He started by reviewing Lucas's company's financial records, looking for any suspicious transactions or connections to the art world.

As he dug deeper, he found that Lucas's company had been involved in several high-profile art deals, often with galleries and auction houses implicated in the fraud scheme Selena had been investigating.

Sam's eyes widened as he realized the scope of Lucas's involvement.

He decided to pay a visit to Lucas's business partner, Mason Brooks, to see if he could shed some light on their business dealings.

Mason was a suave and charming man in his late 40s, with a reputation for being ruthless in business.

"So, Detective," Mason said, "what brings you here today?"

Sam showed him the evidence he had gathered. "I'm investigating the murder of Selena Martin. I believe her father, Lucas, may have been involved."

Mason's expression turned cold. "Lucas? Ha! He's a good man. We've done business with him for years."

Sam sensed that Mason was hiding something. "I'd like to know more about your business dealings with Lucas. Can you walk me through some of these transactions?"

Mason hesitated before speaking. "Well, yes... we've done some deals together. Nothing shady, just normal business."

Sam wasn't convinced.

He noticed a faint scratch on Mason's hand, which seemed out of place.

"Can I ask what caused this scratch?" Sam asked, pointing to the scratch.

Mason looked away nervously. "Oh, just a little accident at home."

Sam's gut told him that Mason was lying.

He decided to dig deeper into the background of Mason and check for any clues.

Detective Sam Taylor decided to investigate Mason Brooks's background and potential connections to Selena or the art world.

He started by reviewing Mason's social media profiles and online presence, looking for any clues that might link him to Selena.

As he scrolled through Mason's Instagram feed, he noticed a post from a few months ago, featuring a painting by Selena.

The caption read: "Just acquired this stunning piece by the talented Selena Martin. Can't wait to display it in my office!"

Sam's eyes widened as he realized that Mason must have been a collector of Selena's work.

He made a mental note to look into Mason's art collection and see if there were any other connections between them.

Next, Sam decided to pay a visit to Mason's office, hoping to get a better sense of their relationship.

When he arrived, Mason greeted him with a warm smile. "Ah, Detective! Come on in."

As they sat down in his office, Sam asked: "So, tell me more about your relationship with Selena. You seem to have been a big fan of her work."

Mason leaned back in his chair. "Yes, I was. She was an incredibly talented artist. I even considered commissioning a piece from her before... well, before everything happened."

Sam sensed that Mason was holding something back. "What do you mean 'before everything happened'? What did you know about Selena's investigation into the art fraud scheme?"

Mason's expression turned guarded. "I didn't know much, just rumors and whispers. But I knew she was getting close to uncovering something big."

Sam's gut told him that Mason was hiding something more significant. He decided to push further.

"Can you tell me more about these rumors and whispers? Anything that might help me understand what happened to Selena?"

Mason hesitated before speaking. "Well... there was talk of a rival artist who was jealous of Selena's success. And then there were whispers of a secret society within the art world..."

Sam's eyes narrowed. A rival artist or a secret society? This case just got a whole lot more complicated.

Detective Sam Taylor decided to review Selena's notebook and diary entries again, looking for any clues about her investigation.

As he flipped through the pages, he noticed a passage that caught his eye:

Selena's Notebook

Today, I received a mysterious package with no return address.

Inside, I found a small painting by an unknown artist.

The style is unmistakable - it's one of the artists involved in the fraud scheme. I'm starting to piece together the puzzle... but I'm scared.

Who is sending me these clues? And why?

Sam's eyes scanned the pages, searching for any other mentions of the painting or the unknown artist. He found a sketch of the painting, along with a note:

I think this might be a clue to the mastermind behind the fraud. But who is it? And why are they trying to frame me?

Sam's mind was racing. Could Selena have been onto something big before she died?

He decided to dig deeper into the painting and see if it led him anywhere.

As he examined the painting more closely, he noticed that the brushstrokes seemed familiar.

Suddenly, a name popped into his head: Mason Brooks, Selena's art dealer.

Could Mason be involved in the fraud scheme?

Sam found one more note in the diary which puzzled him.

Selena's Notebook

I had a strange encounter with dad today.

He was acting nervous and agitated, as if he was hiding something.

I asked him what was wrong, and he told me that he had just received some bad news from his business partner.

I don't know what's going on, but something feels off.

Detective Sam Taylor decided to investigate Lucas Martin, Selena's father, further.

He learned that Lucas had a reputation for being ruthless in his dealings.

As he dug deeper, he discovered that Lucas had been involved in several high-profile lawsuits and had even been accused of embezzlement in the past.

Sam's eyes widened as he read through the documents. Could Selena have been investigating her father's shady dealings?

He wondered if Lucas's business partner, who had received "bad news" from Lucas, might be involved in Selena's murder.

Sam showed him the note from Selena's diary. "What do you know about this? What was your business partner talking about?"

Lucas scoffed. "That? Just a misunderstanding. My business partner was going through a tough time and I was trying to help him out."

Sam raised an eyebrow. "A tough time? What kind of tough time?"

Lucas hesitated before speaking. "Let's just say that my business partner was having some financial difficulties and I was trying to help him get back on his feet."

Sam's eyes narrowed. He didn't believe Lucas's story. He decided to keep digging.

Detective Sam Taylor sat across from Lucas Martin; his eyes locked onto the man's face.

"Mr. Martin, I think it's time we had a little chat about your involvement in the fraud scheme," Sam said, his voice firm but controlled.

Lucas's expression remained calm, but his eyes narrowed slightly. "I don't know what you're talking about, Detective."

Sam pulled out a folder filled with documents. "Don't play dumb, Mr. Martin. We have evidence that links you to the scheme. And we have reason to believe that your daughter was investigating you."

Lucas's mask slipped, and for a moment, Sam saw a glimmer of panic in his eyes.

"What are you talking about?" he repeated, his voice rising.

Sam leaned forward. "Don't lie to me, Mr. Martin. We have records of large transactions between your business and the fraudulent accounts. And we have eyewitnesses who place you at the scene of the crime."

Lucas's face turned red with anger, and for a moment, Sam thought he might actually lose it.

But then, something strange happened. Lucas's expression changed, and he looked almost...sad.

"You're saying that Selena was investigating me?" Lucas asked, his voice heavy with emotion.

Sam nodded. "Yes, Mr. Martin. We believe she was getting close to uncovering the truth."

Lucas sighed, and for a moment, Sam thought he saw a glimmer of guilt in his eyes.

But then, he straightened up and smiled coldly.

"I don't know what you're talking about," Lucas said again.

Sam raised an eyebrow. He didn't believe Lucas's denials for a second.

Detective Sam Taylor decided to search Lucas Martin's office, hoping to find some physical evidence that would link him to the fraud scheme.

As he entered the office, he was met with a elegant and modern space that seemed to scream "I'm a successful businessman."

But Sam's eyes were focused on the task at hand.

He began by searching through Lucas's desk drawers, looking for any documents or records that might incriminate him.

As he rummaged through the files, he found a folder labeled "Personal Matters."
Inside, he discovered a series of letters and emails between Lucas and an unknown person, discussing a secret meeting.

Sam's curiosity was piqued.

Who was this person, and what were they discussing with Lucas?

He continued to search the office, searching for any other clues that might lead him to the truth.

As he searched, he stumbled upon a small notebook hidden behind a bookshelf.

It belonged to Selena Martin, and as Sam flipped through its pages, he saw glimpses of her artistic talent and her struggles as an artist. One entry in particular caught his eye:

I've been feeling so trapped lately.

Dad is always pushing me to make more money and I feel like I'm losing myself in the process.

I wish I could just follow my passion and create art for the sake of art, not just for the money.

Sam felt a pang of sympathy for Selena.

She seemed like a talented and creative person who was suffocating under her father's pressure.

He wondered if her murder was somehow connected to her desire for art and creativity.

Detective Sam Taylor sat across from Lucas Martin, his eyes locked onto the man's face. "Lucas, I need to ask you about some letters and emails I found in your office," Sam said, his voice firm but controlled.

Lucas's expression remained calm, but his eyes narrowed slightly. "What are you talking about?"

Sam pulled out the folder containing the documents.

"These letters and emails are between you and an unknown person. They discuss a secret meeting. Can you tell me who this person is and what you were discussing?"

Lucas's eyes flickered, and for a moment, Sam thought he saw a glimmer of guilt.

"I don't know what you're talking about," Lucas said, his voice evasive.

Sam leaned forward. "Don't lie to me, Lucas. We have evidence that links you to the fraud scheme, and now we have these letters and emails that suggest you were involved in something shady. Tell me the truth."

Lucas's face turned red with anger, but then he seemed to collect himself. "I... I can explain," he said slowly.

"The person I was meeting with was an old friend from college. We were discussing a business opportunity."

Sam raised an eyebrow. "A business opportunity? At a secret meeting?"

Lucas shrugged. "It was just a casual meeting to discuss a potential investment opportunity. Nothing illegal."

Sam wasn't convinced.

He sensed that Lucas was hiding something, but he needed more evidence to prove it.

Detective Sam Taylor leaned forward; his eyes locked onto Lucas Martin's. "Lucas, I'm not buying what you're selling. You're not telling me the whole truth. I need to know more about this business opportunity you were discussing with your college friend."

Lucas's expression turned calculating, and he leaned back in his chair.

"Fine, detective. I'll tell you what I can. But I warn you, it's not what you think it is."

Sam's instincts told him that this was a crucial moment in the investigation.

He leaned in closer, his voice low and even. "What is it then?"

Lucas hesitated, his eyes darting around the room before focusing back on Sam.

"I was discussing a potential investment opportunity with my friend. He has a small art gallery that's been struggling to make ends meet, and he was looking for investors to help him expand his business."

Sam raised an eyebrow. "An art gallery? What does that have to do with Selena's murder?"

Lucas shrugged. "Nothing, I assure you. My friend's gallery is completely unrelated to Selena's work or her murder."

Sam wasn't convinced.

He sensed that Lucas was hiding something, but he couldn't quite put his finger on what it was.

Detective Sam Taylor stood outside the art gallery, his eyes scanning the exterior before turning to Lucas. "So, this is the gallery your friend owns?"

Lucas nodded, leading Sam inside.

The gallery was small, with a handful of paintings on display. The owner, a middle-aged man with a friendly smile, greeted them.

"Ah, Lucas! Good to see you," he said, shaking Lucas's hand. "And this is Detective Taylor, I presume?"

Sam nodded. "That's correct. I'm investigating the murder of Selena Martin."

The owner's expression turned somber. "Ah, yes. Terrible news Lucas. My condolences to you and your family."

Sam pulled out his notebook. "Can you tell me more about Selena's connection to your gallery?"

The owner hesitated before speaking. "Well, Selena was a talented artist. She had shown her work here a few times, and we were considering taking her on as a regular artist."

Sam's eyes narrowed. "But she wasn't working here when she died?"

The owner shook his head. "No, no. She had stopped showing her work here about six months ago. We were going through some financial difficulties, and... well, let's just say it didn't work out between us."

Sam sensed that there was more to the story, but he couldn't quite put his finger on what it was.

Sam leaned forward; his eyes locked onto the owner. "So, you're saying that Selena left the gallery because of financial difficulties?"

The owner nodded. "Yes, that's correct. We were struggling to stay afloat, and Selena was one of our most talented artists. But her prices were too high for us to keep her on. We had to make some tough decisions to stay in business."

Sam's brow furrowed. "I see. And did Selena know about the financial difficulties before she left?"

The owner hesitated before speaking. "Well, I think so. I'm not sure if she knew the full extent of our struggles, but I'm pretty sure she had an idea something was amiss."

Sam made a mental note to look into this further.

He turned back to the owner. "Did Selena mention anything about being upset or threatened by anyone or anything related to the gallery's financial situation?"

The owner shook his head. "No, nothing specific. Just that she was frustrated with the whole situation and felt like she was being held back by us."

Sam's eyes narrowed.

This seemed like a potential motive for Selena's murder, but he couldn't shake the feeling that there was more to it.

Sam left the gallery, his mind whirling with possibilities.

He decided to head back to the precinct to review the evidence and see if they could find any connections between Selena's art and her murder.

As he sat at his desk, he pulled out the folder containing Selena's art portfolio.

He began to flip through the pages, studying each piece carefully.

Some of the artwork was bold and vibrant, while others were more subdued and moodier.

Sam noticed that many of the pieces had themes of confinement, struggle, and escape.

He also noticed that some of the pieces seemed to be dated around the time Selena's financial struggles began.

Sam made a mental note to look into this further.

As he continued to study the artwork, one piece in particular caught his eye.

It was a painting of a small, isolated figure standing on a cliff overlooking a vast, open ocean.

The figure was tiny compared to the vast expanse of blue water, but it seemed to be gazing out at something in the distance with a sense of longing.

Sam felt a shiver run down his spine as he looked at the painting.

It was as if Selena was trying to convey a sense of desperation and isolation.

Sam decided to go back to Selena's apartment and take another look around.

He wanted to see if he had missed anything that might be relevant to the case.

As he entered the apartment, he was struck by the same sense of emptiness he had felt the first time he saw it.

The only sound was the hum of the air conditioner, and the faint scent of paint and turpentine lingered in the air.

Sam began to search the apartment, looking for anything that might give him a lead.

He started in the studio, where he found Selena's easel covered in half-finished canvases.

He examined each one carefully, looking for any clues or hidden messages.

As he turned over one of the canvases, a piece of paper fell out.

It was a receipt from a local art supply store, dated a few days before Selena's death.

Sam's eyes narrowed as he looked at the receipt.

It seemed like Selena had been buying a lot of supplies, but there was no indication of what she was working on.

Sam continued to search the apartment, looking for any other clues.

He found a stack of notebooks and journals hidden away in a drawer.

As he flipped through them, he found that they were filled with sketches and notes about art, as well as cryptic messages and poems.

One entry in particular caught his eye:

I'm trying to create something that will set me free.

Something that will make them see me for who I am.

Sam's eyes narrowed as he read the words.

What did they mean?

Was Selena trying to convey a message about her art, or was she talking about something more personal?

Detective Sam Taylor decided to look into Selena's art project and see if there were any leads on who might have wanted her dead.

He arrived at Selena's studio, a small, cluttered space filled with half-finished paintings and sketches.

As he began to sift through her work, he noticed a series of sketches that seemed to be inspired by the protest movement.

There were drawings of people holding signs, marching in the streets, and making their voices heard.

Sam's eyes landed on one particular sketch that caught his attention - a drawing of a woman with a bold, red hair and a determined expression, holding a sign that read "Justice Now."

Sam's phone buzzed with an incoming text from June.

"Hey, Detective. I found something that might be important. Meet me at the coffee shop down the street."

Sam made his way to the coffee shop and found June waiting for him.

"What is it?" he asked, taking a seat.

June handed him a folder filled with documents.

"I found these in Selena's studio. They appear to be research files for her art project. There's a lot of information on corporations that have been involved in shady dealings."

Sam's eyes scanned the documents, his mind racing with possibilities.

"These could be our break in the case," he said, his excitement growing.

As they reviewed the files together, Sam noticed that one of the corporations listed was Collins Inc., the same company Selena had been investigating.

Detective Sam Taylor's eyes widened as he realized the connection between Selena's art project and Collins Inc.

"This is it," he said, his voice low and urgent. "I need to go back to the office and dig deeper into Collins Inc.'s activities."

June nodded, her eyes shining with determination. "I knew it. Selena was onto something big, and someone didn't want her to expose it."

Sam's mind racing, he stood up, phone already in hand.

"Let's get back to the office and start digging, you might be needed June. We need to know what Selena discovered before she was silenced."

As they left the coffee shop, Sam couldn't shake off the feeling that they were getting close to the truth.

He decided to pay a visit to Alan Collins, this time with a warrant for his records.

When he arrived at Collins Inc., Sam was greeted by a lawyer, who seemed nervous and agitated.

"What do you want, detective?" he asked gruffly.

"I want to see Alan Collins," Sam replied firmly.

The lawyer hesitated before disappearing into the office.

A few minutes later, Collins emerged, his expression smug.

"What can I do for you, detective?" he asked, his voice dripping with condescension.

Sam showed him the documents from Selena's studio.

"We found these in Selena's studio. They seem to suggest that your company has been involved in some shady dealings."

Collins laughed. "These are just baseless accusations. My company is a respected member of this community and I have nothing to hide"

Sam's eyes narrowed. "Respected? You mean corrupt? Because that's what it looks like to me and if you have nothing to hide, then may I have a quick look if you don't mind."

Collins's smile faltered, and for a moment, Sam saw a glimmer of fear in his eyes.

Detective Sam Taylor mind racing with the evidence he had gathered so far.

He knew that he had to search the premises for any evidence of corruption or wrongdoing.

He took a deep breath, nodded to himself, and stepped forward.

As he made his way through the offices, he noticed that everyone seemed nervous and on edge.

They were all typing away on their computers, their eyes darting back and forth like they were waiting for something to happen.

Sam's eyes landed on a young woman with a pierced nose, the same one he had noticed earlier.

She was sitting at a desk, staring at a computer screen with a mixture of fear and determination on her face.

"Hey," Sam said, approaching her desk. "Can I talk to you for a minute?"

The woman looked up, her eyes flashing with surprise. "Uh, sure," she said, getting up from her chair.

Sam pulled out his badge. "I'm Detective Taylor. I'm investigating Selena Martin's murder. Can you tell me what you know about her?"

The woman's eyes dropped, and she nodded. "I... I didn't really know her that well," she said hesitantly.

"But I did see her around sometimes. She was working on a project with...with Alan Collins."

Sam's ears perked up. "What kind of project?"

The woman glanced around nervously before speaking in a low tone. "I don't know what it was exactly, but it seemed like Selena was digging into something deep. She was always scribbling notes and making phone calls. I think she might have been onto something big."

Sam's mind racing, he pulled out his notebook and scribbled some notes. "Do you know anything about Collins Inc.'s financial records? Anything unusual or suspicious?"

The woman hesitated before speaking. "I don't know much about the financial stuff, but I do know that Selena was asking questions about it. She seemed really upset when she found out something."

Sam's eyes locked onto hers. "What did she find out?"

The woman shook her head. "I don't know, but I think it was something big. Selena was always writing in this notebook...she wrote about feeling scared and alone."

Sam's heart went out to Selena as he read through the pages of her notebook.

Detective Sam Taylor sat at his desk, surrounded by stacks of papers and files, trying to make sense of Selena's notebook and diary entries.

As he read through her scribbled notes, he began to piece together a picture of her life.

She had been a fiercely independent and determined individual, driven by a strong sense of justice.

Her notes were filled with quotes from her favorite books and philosophers, and she often wrote about the importance of standing up for what was right.

As he delved deeper into her journal, Sam noticed that Selena had been writing about feeling overwhelmed and isolated.

She spoke about the pressure to conform to societal norms and the fear of being ostracized for speaking out against injustice.

Sam's heart went out to Selena as he read about her struggles.

He couldn't help but wonder if her murder was a result of her courage to speak truth to power.

Back at the station, Sam decided to search Collins Inc.'s financial records for any signs of corruption or wrongdoing.

He spent hours poring over spreadsheets and financial reports, looking for any discrepancies or anomalies.

As he worked, his phone buzzed with an incoming text from June. "Hey, I found something," she said. "I was going through Selena's emails and I found a suspicious transaction from Collins Inc. It looks like they made a large payment to an offshore account."

Sam's eyes widened as he quickly got up from his chair. "That's our break," he exclaimed. "Let me get the forensics team to trace that account."

June nodded. "Hope we get something positive."

As they waited for the results, Sam couldn't help but feel a sense of unease. He knew that Collins Inc. was involved in some shady dealings, but he had no idea what they were capable of.

Detective Sam Taylor sat in front of Selena's computer, trying to crack her password.

He had already gone through her phone and email, but he wanted to see if there were any other clues on her computer.

After a few minutes of trying, the screen flickered to life.

Sam's eyes scanned the desktop, looking for any sign of what Selena had been working on.

He noticed a folder labeled "Project X" and his interest was piqued.

As he opened the folder, he saw a series of documents and spreadsheets.

It looked like Selena had been tracking some kind of financial data, but he wasn't sure what it meant.

Sam's eyes landed on a note that caught his attention. "I think I've found something," he exclaimed. "It looks like Selena was investigating a money laundering scheme involving Collins Inc."

June walked into the room, curious. "What did you find?" she asked.

Sam gestured to the screen. "Selena was onto something big. She was tracking financial transactions and suspecting that Collins Inc. was involved in some shady dealings."

June's eyes widened. "That's huge," she said.

Just then, Selena's diary entry flashed in Sam's mind. "I'm so scared," she had written. "I think they're watching me."

Sam's gut told him that Selena had been getting close to uncovering something big before she was killed.

Detective Sam Taylor walked into the DA's office; a folder full of evidence in hand. "We've made a breakthrough in the Selena Martin case," he said, confident.

The DA looked up from her desk, her expression skeptical. "What have you got?"

Sam laid out the evidence, explaining how Selena had been investigating a money laundering scheme involving Collins Inc.

The DA's eyes widened as she reviewed the documents.

"This is serious," she said. "We need to get a warrant to search their premises."

Sam nodded. "I agree. I think Selena was getting close to uncovering something big before she was killed."

The DA nodded and picked up the phone. "I'll get the warrant issued ASAP."

As they waited for the warrant, Sam couldn't help but think about Selena's diary entries.

He had been going through them, trying to get a better sense of who she was and what drove her.

One entry in particular caught his eye.

Selena's Notebook

Today was a hard day.

I had to confront my boss about the discrepancies in the books.

He just laughed and told me I was being paranoid.

Sam wondered if this was related to her murder. Was she being silenced because she was getting too close to the truth?

The DA hung up the phone, a look of determination on her face. "The warrant is approved. Let's get moving."

Sam and the DA arrived at Collins Inc.'s headquarters, accompanied by a team of forensic experts.

They began searching the premises, looking for any evidence that might link the company to Selena's murder.

As they searched, Sam couldn't shake the feeling that they were being watched.

He glanced around, but saw nothing out of the ordinary.

Detective Sam Taylor sat at his desk, staring at Selena's computer screen as he scrolled through her email and social media accounts.

He was looking for any clues that might lead him to her killer.

As he scrolled, he noticed a message from an unknown sender.

The subject line read "Be careful".

The message itself was cryptic, but it seemed to suggest that Selena was being watched.

Sam's eyes narrowed.

This was the kind of clue that could go either way - it could be a genuine warning from someone who knew something, or it could be a red herring designed to throw him off the scent.

He moved on to her social media accounts, searching for any posts or messages that might give him a lead.

He found a few cryptic messages from an account with no profile picture or name.

The messages were brief and didn't seem to make sense on their own, but they did mention Selena's investigation into Collins Inc.

Sam's gut told him that these messages were important, but he wasn't sure what they meant. He made a note to look into the account further.

As he continued to search, he came across a diary entry that caught his eye.

Selena's Notebook

I'm so tired of being alone.

I feel like I'm the only one who sees what's going on.

I just want someone to believe me.

Sam's heart went out to Selena.

She had been struggling with her investigation, and it seemed like she had been feeling isolated and alone.

Detective Sam Taylor sat at his desk, staring at Selena's computer screen as he scrolled through her email and social media accounts.

He was looking for any clues that might lead him to her killer.

Sam and the DA's team spent hours pouring over Collins Inc.'s financial records, searching for any sign of corruption or wrongdoing.

As they worked, Sam couldn't help but think about Selena's diary entries.

He had been going through them, trying to get a better sense of who she was and what drove her.

One entry in particular caught his eye.

Selena's Notebook

I've been feeling so overwhelmed lately.

Work is consuming me. I feel like I'm losing myself.

Sam wondered if this was related to her murder.

Was she being overwhelmed by her investigation, or was there something more going on in her personal life?

As they searched, they found several discrepancies in Collins Inc.'s financial records.

It looked like the company had been embezzling funds and hiding it through complex accounting schemes.

"This is big," the DA said, her voice low and serious. "We need to get this evidence to the authorities."

Sam nodded, his mind racing with possibilities. "I think things are more complicated," he said.

But as they left the office, Sam couldn't shake the feeling that they were still missing something.

He glanced around, feeling like they were being watched.

Sam and the DA's team arrived at Collins Inc.'s headquarters, determined to confront Alan Collins, the CEO, with the evidence of embezzlement.

As they entered the office, Sam could feel the tension in the air.

Alan Collins looked up from his desk, a mixture of surprise and annoyance on his face. "What's going on here?" he asked gruffly.

Sam held up a folder full of financial documents. "We've been investigating a money laundering scheme involving Collins Inc.," he said firmly. "And we have evidence that you're aware of it."

Alan Collins's expression changed from annoyance to alarm. "I don't know what you're talking about," he said, trying to sound innocent.

Sam smiled grimly. "Don't play dumb, Mr. Collins. We have receipts, bank statements, everything. You're not fooling anyone."

The CEO's eyes darted back and forth between Sam and the DA. For a moment, Sam thought he saw a glimmer of something else there - fear? Guilt?

But then Alan Collins's mask slipped back into place. "I'm just a businessman," he said coolly. "I don't know what you're talking about."

Sam leaned forward; his eyes locked on the CEO. "Listen, Mr. Collins, we know you're involved in this scheme. And we know that Selena Martin was investigating it before she was killed. We want to know what you know about her death."

Alan Collins's face went white, but he said nothing.

Sam and the DA's team searched Alan Collins's office and computer, looking for any evidence of his involvement in the embezzlement scheme and Selena's death.

They found several incriminating documents, including emails and financial records, that linked Alan Collins to the fraud.

As they reviewed the evidence, Sam couldn't help but think about Selena's diary entries. One entry in particular caught his eye.

Selena's Notebook

Dad's been acting strange lately.

I don't know what's going on, but I feel like he's hiding something from me.

Sam wondered if Lucas Martin, Selena's father, was somehow involved in her death.

He made a mental note to speak with him again and see if he had any information about Selena's investigation.

Next, they checked Alan Collins's phone records and found a series of cryptic text messages between him and an unknown number.

The messages were vague, but they seemed to suggest that Alan Collins was trying to cover his tracks.

Sam's mind raced with possibilities.

Who was this unknown number?

Was it a co-conspirator or someone who knew more about Selena's death?

As they continued to investigate, they discovered that Alan Collins had a history of shady business dealings and had been involved in several high-profile lawsuits in the past.

Suddenly, a new theory emerged: what if Alan Collins was involved in a deeper conspiracy?

What if he was working with someone else to cover up their own wrongdoing?

Sam and the DA's team returned to the station, determined to dig deeper into Selena's investigation and her connection to Alan Collins.

They decided to pay a visit to Lucas Martin, Selena's father, to see if he knew anything about her work.

As they arrived at Lucas's home, Sam could sense the tension in the air.

Lucas was pacing back and forth in the living room, his eyes red-rimmed from lack of sleep.

"What's going on?" Sam asked gently.

Lucas stopped pacing and turned to face them. "I don't know what's happening," he said, his voice shaking.

"Selena was investigating something big, I know that much. But she wouldn't tell me what it was."

Sam pulled out Selena's notebook and flipped through the pages. "Can you tell me about this?" he asked, showing Lucas a page with cryptic notes.

Lucas's eyes widened as he recognized the handwriting. "That's Selena's," he said. "But I don't know what it means."

Sam showed him a few more pages, trying to get a sense of what Selena was working on.

As they flipped through the notebook, Sam noticed a recurring theme - Selena seemed to be investigating a connection between Collins Inc. and a local charity.

"Did Selena ever mention anything about Collins Inc. or that charity?" Sam asked.

Lucas hesitated before speaking. "Now that you mention it, yes. She did say something about an investigation into Collins Inc.'s finances. But I didn't think much of it at the time."

Sam's eyes narrowed. "And did you know that Alan Collins was in contact with Selena?"

Lucas's eyes darted back and forth before he spoke. "Yes... we had a dinner together a few weeks ago. He said he was interested in supporting local artists."

Sam sensed a possible connection between Lucas and Alan Collins. "Can you tell me more about that dinner?"

Sam and the DA's team decided to press Lucas for more information about the dinner with Alan Collins. "Can you tell me more about that dinner?" Sam asked, his eyes locked on Lucas's.

Lucas hesitated before speaking. "It was just a casual dinner. Alan came over to discuss Selena's art. He was interested in investing in her work."

Sam's eyes narrowed. "And how did you feel about that?"

Lucas shrugged. "I was skeptical at first, but Alan seemed genuine. He said he wanted to support local artists."

Sam pulled out a photo of Selena from his notebook. "Did Selena mention anything to you about this investment?"

Lucas's eyes clouded. "No... she didn't mention anything specific. But I know she was excited about the possibility of getting funding for her art."

Sam sensed a possible connection between Lucas and Alan Collins. "Did you know that Selena was investigating something related to Collins Inc.'s finances?"

Lucas's expression changed, and he looked away.

"I... I didn't know that. But I did notice that Alan seemed to be getting increasingly agitated when Selena would talk about her investigation."

Sam's eyes locked on Lucas's. "Do you think Alan was involved in whatever Selena was investigating?"

Lucas shook his head. "I don't know... but I do know that Selena was getting closer to the truth. She was always scribbling notes and talking about 'the connections'."

Sam pulled out Selena's notebook and flipped to a page with scribbled notes. "What do you think these notes mean?"

Lucas leaned forward, his eyes scanning the page. "I think they're about a pattern of corruption within Collins Inc. Selena was trying to expose it."

Sam's eyes widened as he connected the dots. "And you think Alan Collins was involved in that corruption?"

Sam left suspicious and decided to come back later and search Lucas's company for any evidence of a potential partnership with Collins Inc.

He arrived at the office and met Lucas again, who seemed nervous.

"What can I do for you, Detective?" Lucas asked, fidgeting with his tie.

"I'm just looking for any information about a potential partnership between your company and Collins Inc.," Sam replied.

Lucas's eyes darted around the room before he spoke.

"I think I remember something. There was a meeting a few months ago... but it was just a casual discussion about a potential merger."

Sam's eyes locked onto Lucas's. "Can you tell me more about that meeting?"

Lucas hesitated before speaking. "It was just Alan Collins and I... we discussed the possibility of combining our companies. But it never went anywhere."

Sam pulled out Selena's notebook and flipped to a page with scribbled notes. "What do you know about this symbol?" he asked, showing Lucas the page.

Lucas's eyes widened. "That's the logo of Collins Inc. But I don't know what it means in the context of Selena's notes."
Sam's mind racing, he decided to investigate further.

He searched Selena's studio and found a sketchbook filled with similar symbols.

As he flipped through the pages, he noticed a specific entry: "The truth is hidden in plain sight".

It seemed Selena was trying to convey a message, but what did it mean?

Sam decided to investigate any other connections between Lucas and Collins Inc.

He spent the next few hours pouring over financial records and corporate documents, trying to find any link between Lucas's company and Collins Inc.

Finally, he found a small note buried in a stack of papers.

It was an email from Lucas to Alan Collins, dated a month before Selena's death.

The subject line read: "Potential Partnership Opportunity".

Sam's eyes scanned the email, his heart racing.

It seemed that Lucas was trying to propose a partnership between his own company and Collins Inc.

The email mentioned a potential merger, but also mentioned that Lucas was hesitant due to "ethical concerns".

Sam's phone rang, breaking the silence. It was Alan Collins himself.

"Detective Taylor, I heard you're investigating my connection to Selena Martin," Alan said, his voice smooth as silk.

"That's right, Mr. Collins," Sam replied. "I'm trying to get to the bottom of her murder."

Alan chuckled. "I'm shocked. Selena was a brilliant artist, but I never thought she'd get involved in anything... untoward."

Sam's ears perked up. "Untoward?"

Alan cleared his throat. "I meant that she was getting close to something big. Something that would ruin her reputation."

Sam's eyes narrowed. "What are you talking about?"

Alan sighed. "Look, Detective, I think it's time we had a chat about Selena's investigation. Meet me at my office tomorrow morning."

Sam could sense that Alan was hiding something.

Sam arrived at Alan Collins's office the next morning, feeling a sense of trepidation.

He had a hunch that Alan was hiding something, and he was determined to get to the bottom of Selena's investigation.

Alan greeted him with a firm handshake. "Detective Taylor, thank you for coming. I think it's time we had a chat about Selena's... passion project."

Sam's eyes narrowed. "What do you mean by 'passion project'?"

Alan smiled. "Selena was working on something big. Something that could change the art world forever. But she was getting close to the truth, and that's why... well, that's why she had to go."

Sam leaned forward. "What are you talking about? What truth?"

Alan leaned back in his chair. "Selena discovered something about Collins Inc.'s finances. Something that would have ruined our reputation if it got out."

Sam's eyes locked onto Alan's. "And you think she was going to expose it?"

Alan nodded. "Yes, but I tried to warn her off. I told her that she was playing with fire, but she refused to listen."

Sam sensed a connection between Alan and Selena's death. "Did you ever see Selena with anyone suspicious around the time of her death?"

Alan hesitated before answering. "Well, now that you mention it... I did see her arguing with someone at the art gallery a few days before her death."
Sam's ears perked up. "Who was it?"

Alan shrugged. "I didn't catch his name, but I remember he was wearing a suit and looked like a businessman."

Sam pulled out his notebook and jotted down the description. "Did you know Lucas Martin, Selena's father?"

Alan nodded. "Oh, yes. We've done business together. He's a good man, but I never thought he'd be involved in anything shady."

Sam raised an eyebrow. "Involved in what?"

Alan leaned forward again. "Look, Detective, I think it's time we cut to the chase. Lucas and I were discussing a potential partnership between our companies when Selena started getting close to the truth."

Sam felt a chill run down his spine. Could Lucas be involved in Selena's murder?

Sam decided to investigate the art gallery where Selena argued with someone suspicious.

He arrived at the gallery, a small, intimate space in the heart of the city.

The owner, a middle-aged woman with a kind smile, greeted him warmly.

"Can I help you, detective?" she asked.

"I'm investigating the murder of Selena Martin," Sam replied. "I understand she argued with someone here a few days before her death."

The owner's expression turned somber. "Yes, poor Selena. She was a brilliant artist. I remember her coming in here, looking upset and frustrated. She was arguing with a man in a suit."

Sam pulled out his notebook. "Can you describe him to me?"

The owner thought for a moment. "Tall, dark hair, piercing blue eyes... he looked like he meant business."

Sam's eyes narrowed.

This sounded like the same description Alan Collins had given him.

"Did you see what they were arguing about?" Sam asked.

The owner hesitated before answering. "It was something about one of Selena's paintings. She was furious, and he was trying to calm her down."

Sam's mind racing with possibilities.

Could this be connected to Selena's investigation?

The case is slowly unfolding, but there are still many questions unanswered.

Selena's notebook is providing some clues, but there is still much more to uncover.

Sam asked the gallery owner if she remembered any details about the painting Selena was arguing about.

The owner thought for a moment before responding.

"It was a small, abstract piece. Selena was working on a new series, and she was really passionate about it. I think it was called... 'League of Twisted Art'."

Sam's eyes lit up.

This might be the new lead they had in the case.

He asked the owner to describe the painting in more detail.

"It was a mix of colors, swirling together to create this... this sense of tension. Selena said it was inspired by her own life, but I don't think she ever told me what specifically."

Sam's mind was racing with possibilities.

Could this painting be connected to Selena's investigation?

And what did Lucas Martin have to do with it?

As he left the gallery, Sam couldn't shake off the feeling that there was more to this case than met the eye.

He decided to pay a visit to Lucas Martin and ask him about his involvement in Selena's investigation.

When he arrived at Lucas's office, he found him pacing back and forth, looking worried.

"Lucas, what do you know about Selena's investigation?" Sam asked bluntly.

Lucas stopped pacing and looked at Sam with a mixture of concern and guilt. "What do you mean? What investigation?"

Sam pulled out his notebook. "We have reason to believe that Selena was investigating something when she died. Something connected to her artwork and Collins Inc.'s finances."

Lucas's expression turned pale. "I had no idea. I would have stopped her if I knew..."

Sam's eyes narrowed. "What do you mean?"

Lucas hesitated before answering. "Selena discovered something about Collins Inc.'s accounting practices. She thought it was illegal and wanted to expose them."

Sam's gut told him that Lucas was hiding something.

Sam pressed Lucas for more information about what Selena discovered and why she wanted to expose Collins Inc.

"Can you tell me more about what Selena found out?" Sam asked, his tone firm but controlled.

Lucas hesitated before speaking. "She... she stumbled upon some irregularities in their financial records. I think she was planning to go to the authorities, but I don't know what she actually discovered."

Sam's eyes locked onto Lucas's. "And why did she want to expose them?"

Lucas sighed. "Selena was a passionate person. She believed in justice and fairness. She thought that Collins Inc.'s actions were wrong and that someone should be held accountable."

Sam's mind was racing with possibilities.

Could this be connected to Selena's murder?

Just then, Sam's phone rang. It was a call from the coroner's office.

"What do you have?" Sam asked, answering the phone.

"We've finished processing Selena's autopsy," the coroner replied.

"There's something unusual... a small, almost imperceptible mark on her hand. It looks like a tiny symbol, almost like a fingerprint."

Sam's eyes narrowed. "Can you send me a picture of the symbol?"

The coroner agreed, and Sam received the image on his phone. It looked like a small, intricate design, but he couldn't quite make out what it was.

Back at the station, Sam showed the symbol to his team to check if anyone has any clues.

"This looks familiar," one colleague said, squinting at the image. "I think I've seen this symbol before... but where?"

Sam's eyes lit up. "I think it might be connected to Selena's art."

Sam showed the symbol to Lucas, hoping he might recognize it.

"Have you ever seen this symbol before?" Sam asked.

Lucas's eyes scanned the symbol, his expression thoughtful.

"Now that you mention it, I think I have. It was on one of Selena's art pieces... a painting she was working on before she died."

Sam's ears perked up. "Do you know what it meant?"

Lucas hesitated before speaking. "I think it was connected to... Project X."

Sam's eyes narrowed. "Project X? What is that?"

Lucas's expression turned guarded. "It was a... a financial scheme, of sorts. Collins Inc. was involved, and Selena was suspicious of their activities. She thought they were involved in money laundering."

Sam's gut told him that Lucas was holding back information. He decided to push further.

"What do you know about Project X?" Sam asked, his tone firm.

Lucas sighed. "Look, I didn't want Selena involved in this. It was dangerous. But she was determined to expose them."

Sam's mind was racing with possibilities. Could this be connected to Selena's murder?

Back at the station, Sam began researching possible connections between the symbol and Collins Inc.'s operations.

He spent hours pouring over financial records and documents, but couldn't find any direct link.

As he was about to leave for the day, he received a call from an anonymous source.

"Detective Taylor," the voice said. "I know what happened to Selena Martin. Meet me at the old warehouse on 7th Main Avenue if you want to know the truth."

The line went dead.

Sam arrived at the old warehouse; his gun drawn.

As he entered the dimly lit building, he saw Daniel Martin, Selena's brother, standing in the shadows.

"What do you know about Selena's death?" Sam asked, his eyes scanning the area.

Daniel stepped forward, his expression grave. "I think I know what happened to her. But I need your help to uncover the truth."

Sam holstered his gun. "What do you mean?"

Daniel handed Sam a folder containing several documents and photographs.

"These are Selena's notes and artwork from her investigation into Collins Inc.'s activities. She discovered a money laundering scheme, codenamed 'Project X'. I think she was getting close to exposing them."

Sam's eyes widened as he flipped through the documents. "This is incredible. But what about the symbol on her hand?"

Daniel's eyes locked onto Sam's. "I think it's a signature. Selena used to sign her art pieces with that symbol. She believed it was a representation of her artistic style, but... I think it was more than that."

Sam's mind racing with possibilities. "What do you mean?"

Daniel hesitated before speaking. "I think Selena discovered a connection between the symbol and Project X. She was going to expose them, but... something happened."

Sam's gut told him that Daniel was holding back information. He decided to push further.

"What else do you know about Project X?" Sam asked, his tone firm.

Daniel sighed. "Look, I didn't want Selena involved in this. It was dangerous. But she was determined to expose them."

Sam's eyes narrowed. "Who is behind Project X?"

Daniel glanced around nervously before speaking in a hushed tone. "I think it's... Collins Inc.'s CEO. He's been using their company for his own gain."

Sam's eyes locked onto Daniel's. "And what about Lucas? Does he know anything about this?"

Daniel shook his head. "No, Dad doesn't know anything about Project X. But... I think Selena was getting close to the truth."

Sam thanked Daniel and decided to confront Alan Collins, CEO of Collins Inc., about Project X.

He decided to re-visit Collins Inc's headquarters with his team, a sleek, modern building in the heart of the city.

As they arrived, Sam could feel a sense of unease. Something didn't feel right.

Collins greeted them in his office, a smug smile on his face. "Detective Taylor, what brings you here today?"

Sam showed Collins the symbol and Selena's notes. "We're here to investigate the murder of Selena Martin, and we believe she was involved in an investigation into your company's activities."

Collins's smile faltered for a moment before he regained his composure. "I don't know what you're talking about. Selena was just an artist, not an investigator."

Sam narrowed his eyes. "Don't play dumb, Mr. Collins. We have evidence that suggests otherwise."

Collins leaned back in his chair. "I'm afraid you're mistaken. Selena was just a talented artist who happened to work for my company on occasion."

Sam's gut told him Collins was hiding something. He decided to push further.

"What do you know about Project X?" Sam asked, his tone firm.

Collins's expression turned cold. "I don't know what you're talking about."

Sam's eyes locked onto Collins's. "Don't lie to me, Mr. Collins. We have evidence that suggests Project X was a money laundering scheme involving your company."

Collins's eyes flashed with anger before he regained his composure. "I don't know what you're talking about. And even if I did, I wouldn't tell you."

Sam felt a surge of frustration. He knew he needed to get more information.

Sam decided to press Collins for more information, using whatever means necessary.

He knew that Collins was hiding something, and he was determined to get to the truth.

"Look, Collins," Sam said, his voice firm. "We have evidence that suggests Project X was a money laundering scheme involving your company. And I think Selena was getting close to exposing it."

Collins's expression remained calm, but Sam could see the faintest hint of panic in his eyes. "I've told you, Detective, I don't know what you're talking about."

Sam leaned forward; his eyes locked onto Collins's. "Don't play dumb with me, Collins. I've seen Selena's artwork, and I know she was onto something big. And I think it's connected to Project X."

Collins's eyes darted around the room before landing back on Sam's face. "Fine," he said, his voice dripping with reluctance.

"If you must know, Project X was a... a side project of sorts. A way for us to generate extra revenue."

Sam's grip on his notebook tightened. "By selling fake art to rich people?"

Collins's expression turned guarded. "That's...that's not exactly what I meant. It was more like...a way to create value where none existed."

Sam raised an eyebrow. "By creating fake art?"

Collins hesitated before speaking. "Yes, okay? We created fake art pieces and sold them to collectors at inflated prices. It was all very legal and above board."

Sam's eyes narrowed. "And Selena knew about this?"

Collins nodded slowly. "Yes, she did. And she was going to expose us."

Sam felt a surge of anger at the thought of Selena being silenced. He knew he had to keep pushing.

"What happened to her?" he demanded.

Collins's expression turned cold. "I don't know what you're talking about."

Sam knew that Collins was lying again. He decided to take a different approach.

Sam decided to ask Collins more questions about Project X. He leaned back in his chair, his eyes locked onto Collins's.

"So, Collins, tell me more about Project X," Sam said, his voice firm. "How did it work?"

Collins hesitated before speaking. "Well, as I said, it was a way for us to generate extra revenue. We would create fake art pieces and sell them to collectors at inflated prices."

Sam's brow furrowed. "Fake art pieces? You mean you were creating art that wasn't actually created by the artists themselves?"

Collins nodded. "Yes, that's correct. We would buy art from emerging artists at a low price and then sell it to collectors at a much higher price. It was all very legal and above board."

Sam raised an eyebrow. "And Selena knew about this?"

Collins nodded again. "Yes, she did. And she was going to expose us."

Sam's eyes narrowed. "Why didn't you just sorted by talking to her? Why did you have to kill her?"

Collins's expression turned cold. "I didn't order her death, Detective. I swear it."

Sam's grip on his notebook tightened. "Then who did?"

Collins shrugged. "I don't know. But I think it's clear that someone within the company wanted Selena silenced."

Sam's mind raced with possibilities. He decided to ask Collins another question.

"What do you know about Selena's last days?" he asked.

Collins thought for a moment before speaking. "She was getting closer and closer to the truth, I'm sure of it. She was asking too many questions and poking her nose into places it didn't belong."

Sam's eyes locked onto Collins's. "What did she discover?"

Collins hesitated before speaking. "I don't know exactly, but I think she may have found out about our plans to expand Project X to other cities."

Sam's eyes narrowed. "What plans?"

Collins shrugged. "Just plans to expand our reach and increase our profits."

Sam felt a surge of frustration. He knew he needed to get more information.

Sam decided to ask Collins more questions about the plans to expand Project X.

He leaned forward in his chair, his eyes locked onto Collins's.

"What exactly did you plan to do with the expanded Project X?" Sam asked.

Collins's expression turned guarded. "I'm not at liberty to discuss that, Detective. But I can tell you that it was all above board and legal."

Sam raised an eyebrow. "Above board and legal? You mean like selling fake art to rich people?"

Collins's eyes narrowed. "That's not what I meant, Detective. But yes, selling art to collectors who were willing to pay top dollar for it."

Sam's grip on his notebook tightened. "And how did Selena fit into this plan?"

Collins hesitated before speaking. "She was...involved with the project, Detective. She was supposed to be one of the lead artists."

Sam's eyes widened. "So, she was going to create fake art for you to sell?"

Collins nodded. "Yes, that's correct."

Sam felt a surge of anger at the thought of Selena being used by Collins and his company. He decided to ask more questions.

"What kind of art was she supposed to create?" he asked.

Collins thought for a moment before speaking. "She was supposed to create...impressionist pieces. You know, the kind of thing that would appeal to the wealthy collectors we were targeting."

Sam's eyes narrowed. "And what kind of pieces did she create instead?"

Collins shrugged. "I don't know, Detective. But I do know

that she was getting closer and closer to the truth. And then...she disappeared."

Sam felt a chill run down his spine. He knew he needed to get more information.

Sam decided to search the company's offices for any physical evidence that might lead them to Selena's killer.

He and his team combed through every room, searching for anything out of place or suspicious.

As they searched, Sam couldn't help but think about Selena's notebook entries.

He had a sense that she was trying to tell him something, but what?

He found a piece of paper on the floor that caught his eye.

It was a sketch of a painting, but it was unlike anything he had ever seen before.

The colors were vibrant and swirling, like a stormy sea.

"Hey, look at this," Sam said to his team. "I think this might be Selena's work."

They examined the sketch more closely, trying to figure out what it meant. But as they did, Sam's phone rang. It was Lucas Martin, Selena's father.

"What did you find?" Lucas asked, his voice anxious.

"We're still searching the office," Sam said. "But I think we might have found something important. Can you come down here and take a look?"

Lucas agreed, and soon he arrived at the office.

Together, they examined the sketch and discussed its possible significance.

"I think this might be a clue," Sam said. "It looks like Selena was trying to tell us something about Project X."

Lucas's eyes narrowed. "What do you mean?"

Sam hesitated before speaking. "I think she might have discovered something about the project that she didn't like. And I think someone might have silenced her to keep it quiet."

Lucas's face turned pale. "Oh no. I had no idea."

Sam and his team continued to search the office, focusing on any connections to Project X. They combed through files, computers, and papers, looking for anything that might lead them to Selena's killer.

As they searched, Sam couldn't help but think about Selena's notebook entries.

He had a sense that she was trying to tell him something, but what?

He found a folder labeled "Project X - Confidential" and opened it.

Inside, he found a series of documents outlining the project's goals and plans.

But what caught his eye was a memo from Alan Collins himself, stating that Selena had been making progress on a new piece for the project.

Sam's eyes narrowed.

This was the first time they had heard that Selena was working on a new piece for Project X.

He wondered what it could be and why it was so important.

Next to the memo was a photograph of Selena, taken in her studio.

She was standing in front of an easel, holding a paintbrush and gazing at her work with a look of intense concentration.

Sam felt a pang of sadness.

This was the last time anyone had seen Selena alive.

He turned to his team. "We need to talk to Alan Collins again," he said. "I think he knows more than he's letting on."

Sam decided to ask Collins about Selena's last few days before her disappearance.

"Can you tell me more about Selena's last few days?" Sam asked, his eyes locked onto Collins's.

Collins thought for a moment before speaking.

"Well, she was getting more and more agitated as the days went by. She was having trouble sleeping and seemed really anxious all the time."

Sam's grip on his notebook tightened. "Did she say anything to you about what was bothering her?"

Collins hesitated before speaking. "No, she didn't. But I could tell something was eating at her. She was distant and withdrawn, and she wouldn't even look at me when I talked to her."

Sam's eyes narrowed. "And did she say anything about leaving the company?"

Collins nodded. "Yes, she did. She told me that she was going to leave and that she wouldn't be coming back."

Sam's heart skipped a beat. "Did she say why?"

Collins shook his head. "No, she didn't. But I knew something was wrong. I tried to talk to her, but she just shut me down."

Sam felt a surge of frustration. He knew he needed to get more information.

Sam decided to ask Collins if he knows of anyone who might have wanted Selena dead.

"I'm going to be blunt, Collins," Sam said. "I think someone might have wanted Selena dead. Do you know of anyone who might have had a motive?"

Collins's expression turned serious. "I don't know of anyone specific, Detective. But I do know that Selena was getting closer and closer to the truth about Project X. And I know that there were some people who didn't want her to find out what we were really doing."

Sam's eyes narrowed. "What do you mean?"

Collins leaned in; his voice low. "I mean that Project X was a way for us to make a lot of money. And some people were willing to do whatever it took to keep that from happening."

Sam's grip on his notebook tightened. "And you think one of those people might have killed Selena?"

Collins nodded. "I do. And I think they might still be out there, watching us, waiting for their chance to strike again."

Sam felt a surge of determination. He was going to get to the bottom of this case.

Sam decided to investigate the art market and see if they could find any leads on who might have wanted Selena dead.

He started by visiting some of the local art galleries and dealers, showing them Selena's work and asking if they had any information about her or her art.

Most of them seemed to know her, but none of them had any idea what had happened to her.

As he was leaving one gallery, a young artist approached him. "Hey, you're looking for Selena Martin, right?" she asked.

Sam nodded. "That's right. Do you know anything about her?"

The artist hesitated before speaking. "I didn't know her well, but I saw her around the art scene. She was a talented artist, but she was also really struggling. I heard she was working on some new project, but I don't know what it was."

Sam's eyes lit up. "Do you know what kind of project it was?"

The artist shook her head. "No, sorry. But I did hear that she was getting close to exposing something big. Something that could ruin a lot of reputations."

Sam's grip on his notebook tightened. This was the new lead they had gotten.

Sam decided to investigate the art world further to see if anyone else knows what Selena was working on.

He spent the next few days visiting various art galleries and studios, showing Selena's work and asking if anyone had any information about her or her art.

Most of them seemed to know her, but none of them had any idea what she was working on.

One gallery owner, a woman seemed particularly nervous when Sam mentioned Selena's name.

"Oh, yes, Selena," she said. "She was a talented artist, but she was also very... sensitive. She had a way of pushing boundaries that not everyone appreciated."

Sam's eyes narrowed. "What do you mean by that?"

The owner hesitated before speaking. "I mean that Selena wasn't afraid to speak her mind. She was passionate about her art, and she wasn't afraid to take risks. But sometimes that passion could get her into trouble."

Sam's mind was racing with possibilities. Was Selena's passion for art what got her killed?

Sam decided to ask Collins if he knows of any specific individuals who might have been involved in Selena's murder.

"Can you think of anyone who might have had a personal vendetta against Selena?" Sam asked, his eyes locked onto Collins's.

Collins thought for a moment before speaking.

"Well, there was one person who came to mind. His name is Bruce Evans. He's an art collector and a rival of mine in the business. He's always been jealous of my success and has tried to sabotage me in the past."

Sam's ears perked up. "What makes you think he might have been involved in Selena's murder?"

Collins leaned in; his voice low. "I saw him arguing with Selena at a gallery opening a few weeks ago. They were going at it over one of her paintings, and I could tell it was getting pretty heated. I didn't think much of it at the time, but now I wonder if maybe it was more than just an argument."

Sam's eyes narrowed. "I'll look into it. Do you have any idea where I might be able to find Bruce?"

Collins nodded. "Yeah, he owns a gallery on the other side of town. I'm sure he'll be happy to talk to you."

Sam stood up, his mind racing with possibilities. He had a lead to follow up on.

Sam decided to investigate Selena's paintings and see if she left behind any clues about her suspicions about Project X.

He arrived at the gallery and began to scan the room, taking in the various paintings on display.

He noticed that one of the paintings, an abstract piece with bold brushstrokes and vivid colors, seemed to be slightly askew on the wall.

He walked over to investigate and saw that the frame was slightly loose.

He carefully removed the painting from the wall and examined it more closely.

Inside the frame, he found a small piece of paper with a message scrawled in red ink:

"They're all fake. Look closer."

Sam's eyes narrowed as he turned the paper over in his hand. What did Selena mean? Was this a reference to her own artwork or something more?

He decided to take a closer look at the other paintings in the gallery, seeing if there were any other clues or hidden messages.

As he examined the paintings, he noticed that several of them seemed to be subtly altered or retouched.

The brushstrokes were slightly different, the colors were slightly off.

It was as if Selena had been working on them, trying to convey a message or leave a clue.

Sam's mind was racing as he tried to decipher what Selena was trying to say. Was she trying to tell him that Project X was selling fake art? Or was there something more sinister at play?

Sam decided to investigate Selena's financial records and see if there were any transactions related to Project X.

He obtained a copy of Selena's financial records and began to sift through them, looking for any suspicious activity.

After several hours of searching, he finally found a small transaction that caught his eye.

It was a payment from an anonymous source to Selena's bank account, in the amount of $10,000.

The payment was dated just a few weeks before her death.

Sam's eyes narrowed as he wondered what this payment could be for. Was it a payment for one of her paintings? Or was it something more sinister?

He decided to pay a visit to Lucas Martin, Selena's father, to ask him about the payment.

As he arrived at Lucas's office, he could sense that Lucas was nervous. "What can I do for you, Detective?" he asked, trying to sound calm.

"While investigating your daughter's death," Sam replied and paused. "I found a suspicious transaction in her financial records. Can you tell me anything about it?"

Lucas's eyes widened. "I don't know what you're talking about."

Sam pulled out the transaction record and handed it to Lucas. "This is a payment from an anonymous source to your daughter's account. Can you tell me who made this payment?"

Lucas looked at the record, his eyes scanning the page before looking up at Sam. "I... I don't know," he said hesitantly. "But I think I might be able to find out."

In the meanwhile, Sam went through Selena's diary and found something.

Selena's Notebook

I've been feeling so trapped lately, like I'm stuck in a rut.

I've been trying to break free from my comfort zone and take risks with my art, but it's hard when you're afraid of failure.

I've been thinking about my childhood a lot lately, and how my father always pushed me to be perfect.

I think that's why I've always felt like I need to be perfect too. But it's exhausting.

I want to be free from all of this pressure and just create for the sake of creating.

Sam wondered on the entry which gives more insight into Selena's struggles with perfectionism and her relationship with her father. It also raises questions about her feelings of being trapped and her desire for freedom.

Sam decided to ask Lucas if he knew anything about Project X or its connections to Selena.

"Lucas, I need to ask you something," Sam said, his tone firm but polite. "I know you're still grieving, but can you share more information about Project X."

Lucas's expression changed from sadness to surprise. "Project X? Does it relate anything with Selena's death?"

"I found a payment from an anonymous source in her financial records," Sam explained. "I think it might be connected to Project X. Can you tell me more about it?"

Lucas hesitated, then shook his head. "No, I told you everything I've heard of Project X, which I earlier thought as a rumor."

Sam raised an eyebrow. "A rumor?"

Lucas nodded. "Yeah, I heard it was a black-market art operation. They were selling fake art to rich people who didn't care about the authenticity."

Sam's eyes narrowed. "Do you think Selena was involved with them?"

Lucas shook his head again. "No, no way. Selena was a talented artist. She would never compromise her integrity like that."

Sam wasn't so sure. He decided to keep investigating and see if he could find any more connections between Selena and Project X.

Sam decided to ask Lucas if he knew anyone who might have been involved with Project X apart from Collins.

"Lucas, can you think of any other name who might have been involved with Project X except Collins?" Sam asked, his eyes scanning the room.

Lucas thought for a moment before shaking his head.

"No, I don't know anyone else who would be involved with something like that. But I do know someone who might know more about it."

"Who's that?" Sam asked, his interest piqued.

"Bruce Evans," Lucas replied. "He's a rival art dealer. He's always been jealous of my daughter's talent and success. He might know something more about Project X."

Sam's eyes narrowed. "I'll look into him," he said.

Meanwhile, Sam decided to look into the background of the anonymous source who made the payment to Selena's account.

After some digging, he discovered that the payment was made from an account in the name of Bruce Evans, the rival art dealer.

Sam's eyes narrowed as he wondered what kind of connection Bruce Evans could have had with Selena.

Was he a patron of her art? Or was there something more sinister at play?

He decided to pay a visit to Bruce Evans's gallery, hoping to get some answers.

As he arrived at the gallery, he was greeted by Bruce himself.

"What can I do for you, Detective?" Bruce asked, his voice dripping with condescension.

"I'm investigating the death of Selena Martin," Sam replied. "I understand that you made a payment to her account recently. Can you tell me about that?"

Bruce smiled, his eyes glinting with amusement. "Ah, yes. Selena was a talented artist. I was simply showing my appreciation for her work."

Sam raised an eyebrow. "Appreciation? For $10,000?"

Bruce shrugged. "It was a generous gesture, I assure you. She needed it."

Sam's instincts told him that there was more to the story. He decided to press on.

"Can you tell me about your relationship with Selena?" he asked.

Bruce chuckled. "We were acquaintances, nothing more. We would occasionally discuss art and... other things."

Sam's eyes narrowed. "Other things?"

Bruce leaned in, his voice taking on a conspiratorial tone. "Let's just say that Selena and I shared certain...interests. But I assure you, our relationship was purely professional."

Sam wasn't convinced. He thanked Bruce for his time and left the gallery, his mind racing with possibilities.

Sam decided to investigate Selena's connections to other art dealers or collectors who may have had dealings with Project X.

He spent the next few days tracking down leads and conducting interviews, but came up empty-handed.

As he was leaving the art district, he received a call from an anonymous source claiming to have information about Selena's dealings with Project X.

The source wanted to meet at a coffee shop on the outskirts of town.

Sam arrived at the coffee shop and saw a figure waiting for him in the corner. It was a woman with short, curly hair and a nervous smile.

"I'm Diana," she said, extending her hand. "I used to work with Selena at Collins Inc. I think I might know something about Project X."

Sam's eyes lit up. "What do you know?"

Diana hesitated before speaking. "I overheard Selena and Alan Collins talking about Project X a few months ago. They were discussing how they could use it to make a lot of money."

Sam's eyes narrowed. "Did they say how they planned to do it?"

Diana shook her head. "No, but I know they were going to meet with some wealthy collectors to show them some...art pieces."

Sam's mind racing. "Do you know who these collectors were?"

Diana thought for a moment before speaking. "One of them was a man named...Vincent Alvarez. He's a rich collector who loves modern art."

Sam's eyes locked onto Diana's. "Did Selena say anything else about Vincent Alvarez?"

Diana nodded. "She was worried about him, actually. She said he was trying to pressure her into creating more art for him, but she didn't want to compromise her style."

Sam's instincts told him that Vincent Alvarez might be involved in Selena's death. He decided to pay him a visit.

Meanwhile, Sam went through Selena's diary.

Selena's Notebook

I've been feeling so overwhelmed lately, like I'm drowning in expectations from all sides.

My father wants me to paint more commercial pieces, Alan wants me to create something that will make us both rich, and I just want to create something true to myself.

I've been thinking about my childhood a lot lately, and how my parents always pushed me to be perfect.

I think that's why I feel so trapped now, because I'm trying to live up to their expectations instead of my own.

I wish I could break free from all of this and just be myself.

Sam felt Selena's struggles with feeling trapped and her desire to be true to herself. It also raises questions about her relationships with her parents and Alan Collins.

Sam decided to look into the background of Diana and her possible motives for coming forward.

He discovered that Diana was a former employee of Collins Inc., where she worked as a curator for several years before leaving the company.

She had been friends with Selena, but their friendship had cooled off in the past year.

Sam paid a visit to Diana's apartment, where she was nervous and fidgety. "I'm just glad I could help with the case," she said. "I feel terrible about what happened to Selena."

Sam pulled out a photo of Selena's art studio. "Can you tell me more about this studio? Did Selena ever talk to you about her work here?"

Diana's eyes scanned the photo before speaking. "Oh, yeah. She loved that studio. She would spend hours in there, painting and experimenting with new techniques. But...I don't think it was all good times, though."

Sam raised an eyebrow. "What do you mean?"

Diana hesitated before speaking. "Selena was struggling a lot with her art. She was trying to please her father and Alan Collins, but it was taking a toll on her. She would get really frustrated and depressed sometimes."

Sam's eyes narrowed. "Did you ever notice anything suspicious around the studio?"

Diana thought for a moment before speaking. "Actually, yes. I saw someone lurking around the studio a few times. I never saw their face, but they seemed really interested in Selena's work."

Sam's instincts told him that this could be a lead worth pursuing.

He thanked Diana for her time and left her apartment, his mind racing with possibilities.

Sam decided to explore Selena's childhood and relationships with her parents to see if there were any clues about her death.

He visited Lucas Martin, Selena's father, at his art gallery.

Lucas was a successful artist himself, known for his avant-garde style.

He was also a bit of a perfectionist, which Sam sensed might have influenced Selena's struggles with her own artistic identity.

"Selena was always a sensitive child," Lucas said, looking at old family photos.

"She was a bit of a dreamer, always getting lost in her own world. I wanted her to be more grounded, to focus on her craft."

Sam's eyes narrowed. "Did you ever pressure her to conform to your expectations?"

Lucas hesitated before speaking. "Maybe a little. I wanted her to be the best, just like me. But I never meant to hurt her."

Sam thanked Lucas for his time and left the gallery, feeling like he was getting closer to understanding Selena's motivations.

Sam arrived at Vincent Alvarez's mansion; a grand estate nestled in the hills overlooking the city.

He was greeted by a butler who showed him to a luxurious study.

Vincent Alvarez, a tall, imposing man with a stern face, looked up from behind his desk. "Can I help you, Detective?"

Sam flashed his badge. "I'm investigating the death of Selena Martin. I understand she was involved with you in some capacity."

Vincent's expression turned cold. "Yes, we were acquaintances. She was a talented artist, but her work was...unsophisticated."

Sam's eyes narrowed. "Unsophisticated? What do you mean?"

Vincent shrugged. "She was trying to create something new, something bold. But her style was too raw, too...unrefined."

Sam sensed that Vincent was hiding something. He decided to push further.

"What did you talk about when you met with Selena?"

Vincent's eyes flickered for a moment before he spoke. "We discussed art, of course. She was looking for feedback on her work."

Sam's instincts told him that Vincent was lying. He decided to keep pushing.

"Did Selena ever mention anything about Project X to you?"

Vincent's expression changed, becoming more guarded. "I don't know what you're talking about."

Sam's eyes locked onto Vincent's. "Don't lie to me, Mr. Alvarez. I know Selena was involved with Project X. Did she tell you anything about it?"

Vincent's eyes dropped, and for a moment, Sam thought he saw a glimmer of fear. But then the mask slipped back into place.

"I don't know what you're talking about," Vincent repeated.

Sam wasn't convinced.

He thanked Vincent for his time and left the mansion, his mind racing with possibilities.

Sam decided to look into Vincent Alvarez's alibi for the time of Selena's death.

He paid a visit to the local police station and obtained a copy of Vincent's statement from the night of Selena's murder.

According to Vincent, he had been at a charity gala at the city's upscale museum from 8pm to 11pm, where he was one of the main sponsors.

However, Sam noticed that Vincent's alibi was shaky at best.

There were no witnesses who could vouch for his presence at the gala, and the museum's security cameras didn't show him entering or leaving the building during that time.

Sam decided to pay a visit to the museum and investigate further.

He spoke with the event coordinator, who seemed nervous and evasive when questioned about Vincent's presence.

"I don't remember him being there," she said. "But I'm sure he was. He was supposed to be one of our main sponsors."

Sam thanked her for her time and left the museum, his mind racing with possibilities.

He couldn't shake the feeling that Vincent was hiding something.

Sam decided to confront Vincent Alvarez with the new evidence and accuse him of murder.

He arrived at Vincent's mansion, feeling a sense of determination and purpose.

Vincent answered the door, looking calm and collected. "Can I help you, Detective?"

Sam flashed his badge. "I need to ask you some more questions about Selena Martin's death."

Vincent raised an eyebrow. "What's this about?"

"You've been lying to me, Vincent," Sam said, his voice firm. "I have reason to believe you were not at the charity gala that night. I think you're hiding something."

Vincent smiled, a cold, calculating smile. "I don't know what you're talking about."

Sam pulled out a photo from his pocket. "This is a security camera photo from the museum's parking garage. It shows you leaving the building around 10pm that night. Care to explain?"

Vincent's expression faltered for a moment before he regained his composure. "I must have forgotten about that," he said, his voice dripping with insincerity.

Sam wasn't convinced. "I think you're hiding something, Vincent. And I think you're involved in Selena's murder."

Vincent shrugged. "I'm just an art critic, Detective. I had nothing to do with Selena's death."

Sam's instincts told him that Vincent was lying, but he needed more concrete evidence before he could make an arrest.

Sam decided to search Vincent's mansion for more evidence.

He obtained a warrant and entered the mansion, accompanied by a team of forensic experts.

As they began to search the mansion, Sam noticed that Vincent seemed nervous and agitated. "What are you doing?" he asked, his voice trembling.

"Just searching for evidence, Vincent," Sam replied. "We're trying to find out what happened to Selena Martin."

The search turned up several suspicious items, including a set of fake art authentication certificates and a ledger with records of fake art sales.

It seemed that Vincent was indeed involved in Project X, selling fake art to wealthy collectors.

But as Sam and his team continued to search the mansion, they found something even more disturbing.

A hidden room in the basement, containing a collection of Selena's artworks, all of which seemed to be... changed.

The paintings and sculptures were all twisted and distorted, with strange symbols etched into the surface.

It was as if Selena had been experimenting with her art, trying to convey a message or tell a story.

Sam's gut told him that this was important. He needed to know what Selena was trying to say with her art.

Sam decided to question Vincent about the hidden room and the altered artwork.

He quickly called a team of forensic experts.

Vincent was pacing back and forth in the living room, looking agitated. "What is it that you want to know?" he asked, his voice tight.

Sam pulled out a photo of the hidden room. "This. What do you know about this?"

Vincent's eyes widened. "Where did you get that?"

"It's a hidden room in your basement," Sam replied. "And these... they're Selena's artwork, aren't they?"

Vincent nodded slowly. "Yes. I... I didn't know she was working on anything like this."

Sam raised an eyebrow. "You didn't know? Or you didn't want to know?"

Vincent sighed. "I was trying to help her with her career. I thought this was a way to make her famous."

Sam's eyes narrowed. "By selling her fake art to rich people?"

Vincent shook his head. "No, no, of course not! I would never do that!"

Sam wasn't convinced. He knew that Vincent was involved in Project X, and he suspected that he was involved in Selena's murder.

"We know about Project X," Sam said, his eyes locked on Vincent's. "We know you were involved in selling fake art to rich people."

Vincent shifted uncomfortably in his chair. "I... I didn't mean for it to go that far," he stammered. "I just wanted to make a quick buck."

Sam's expression turned cold. "You used your connection with Selena to sell her fake art, didn't you?"

Vincent nodded slowly. "Yes... I'm sorry. I didn't mean for her to get hurt."

Sam's anger boiled over. "You're sorry? You're sorry? You're the one who killed her!"

Vincent looked up, shocked. "What? No! I didn't kill her!"

Sam's eyes narrowed. "We'll see about that. We'll investigate your alibi for the time of Selena's death."

Vincent's face turned pale. "I... I was with my business partner, Alan Collins."

Sam raised an eyebrow. "Alan Collins? The CEO of Collins Inc?"

Vincent nodded. "Yes... he can vouch for me."

Sam's gut told him that something wasn't right. He decided to pay Alan Collins a visit.

Sam decided to investigate Vincent further, specifically about Selena's relationships with her father and Alan Collins.

Vincent seemed nervous, fidgeting in his seat. "What do you want to know?" he asked, trying to hide his guilt.

Sam pulled out a photo of Selena's artwork. "We found this in her studio. It seems like she was working on a series of pieces about her relationships with her father and Alan Collins. Do you know anything about this?"

Vincent hesitated, then nodded slowly. "Yes... I did know about it. Selena confided in me about her struggles with her father. She felt like he was suffocating her, trying to control her artistic style."

Sam's eyes narrowed. "And what about Alan Collins? Did she confide in you about him too?"

Vincent shifted uncomfortably. "Yes... she did. She was frustrated with him, feeling like he was using her for his own gain. He would often try to manipulate her into creating art that would sell well, rather than what she truly wanted to create."

Sam's suspicions grew. "Do you think Alan Collins had anything to do with Selena's death?"

Vincent shook his head. "I don't think so... but I did notice that Selena was getting more and more withdrawn around him towards the end. She was distant, like she was scared of him or something."

Sam made a mental note to investigate Alan Collins further.

Sam decided to investigate Lucas Martin's behavior towards Selena, to see if it was abusive or controlling. He and his team went to Lucas's office, ready to ask some tough questions.

Lucas was defensive from the start. "I didn't do anything to hurt my daughter," he said, his voice rising.

Sam pulled out a copy of Selena's diary. "We've found some entries that suggest otherwise. It seems like you were pressuring her to create art that would make you proud, rather than allowing her to follow her own creative vision."

Lucas's face turned red with anger. "That's not true! I was just trying to help her succeed!"

Sam's eyes narrowed. "Help her succeed? Or control her? We've also found evidence that you were involved in Project X, selling fake art to rich people. Did you use Selena's talents for your own gain?"

Lucas's expression changed from anger to guilt. "I... I didn't mean for it to go that far. I just wanted to make a quick buck."

Sam's gut told him that Lucas was hiding something. "I think you're not telling us the whole truth," he said. "We'll need to investigate further."

Sam and his team searched Lucas's office and home for evidence of his involvement in Project X.

They found a hidden folder on his computer containing emails and documents related to the fake art scheme.

One email in particular caught Sam's eye:

Subject: Meeting with Alan Collins

Dear Lucas,

I've received the new batch of fake art pieces from Selena. They're looking great, as always. I've set up a meeting with some potential buyers for next week. Let me know if you're free to join us.

Best,
Alan

Sam's eyes narrowed.

This seemed like concrete evidence that Alan Collins was involved in the scheme, and that Lucas was aware of it.

Sam and his team continued to search Lucas's office and home, looking for any connection between him and Project X.

They found a folder labeled "Personal Correspondence" containing letters from Selena to her father.

The first letter was from when Selena was a teenager:

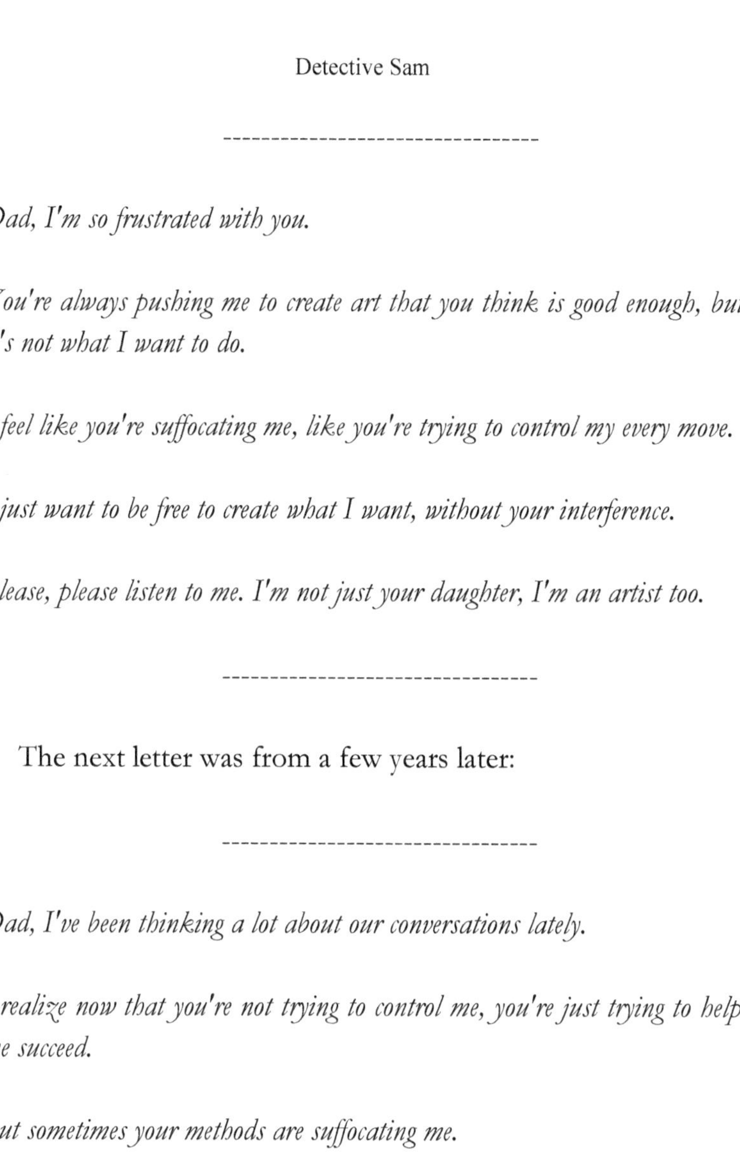

Dad, I'm so frustrated with you.

You're always pushing me to create art that you think is good enough, but it's not what I want to do.

I feel like you're suffocating me, like you're trying to control my every move.

I just want to be free to create what I want, without your interference.

Please, please listen to me. I'm not just your daughter, I'm an artist too.

The next letter was from a few years later:

Dad, I've been thinking a lot about our conversations lately.

I realize now that you're not trying to control me, you're just trying to help me succeed.

But sometimes your methods are suffocating me.

I feel like I'm losing myself in all the pressure and expectations.

Can we find a way to compromise?

Can we find a way for me to be the artist I want to be, without you holding me back?

Sam's eyes widened as he read the letters. It seemed that Selena's relationship with her father was complex, with feelings of frustration and desperation on both sides.

Sam decided to investigate Selena's relationship with Alan Collins further, to see if she was aware of the fake art scheme.

He and his team went to Selena's apartment, searching for any evidence that might link her to the project.

As they searched, they found a folder filled with documents and receipts related to Project X.

It seemed like Selena had been aware of the scheme, but had been using it as a way to fund her own art projects.

The question was, did she know about the fake art being sold, or was she just oblivious?

Sam's team also found a torn paper from Selena's diary:

I've been feeling so guilty about this.

I know it's wrong, but Alan has been promising me that it will help me get my art career off the ground.

He says it's a way to make a lot of money quickly, and then I can focus on my real art.

But deep down, I know it's not right.

I feel like I'm compromising my integrity.

I've been trying to find ways to get out of this situation, but Alan is really good at manipulating me.

He makes me feel like I owe him, like I'm in debt to him.

I don't know what to do.

This entry suggests that Selena was aware of the fake art scheme, but was torn between her desire to advance her art career and her moral objections to the scheme.

Sam decided to search Selena's computer and phone records for any evidence of communication with Alan Collins or other Project X members.

His team found a series of emails and texts between Selena and Alan, discussing the sale of her art pieces to wealthy collectors.

One email in particular caught their attention:

Hey Selena, I've got a potential buyer lined up for your latest piece. They're willing to pay top dollar, but I need you to make some minor changes to the artwork before they'll commit. Just a few brushstrokes here and there. I know it's not ideal, but it'll be worth it in the long run.

The team also found a text message from Alan to Selena:

Hey Em, just wanted to remind you that you owe me one. Don't forget who got you into this industry.

These communications suggested that Selena was aware of the fake art scheme, and was complicit in it.

But was she just an unwitting participant, or did she know the full extent of the scam?

Sam's team continued to search for any other evidence of Selena's involvement in Project X.

They found a receipt from a local art supply store, with a note on the back that read:

To: Selena W.
From: Alan J.
For: Art supplies for 'Project X'

Amount: $500

Date: 02/15/2023

This receipt suggested that Selena had been purchasing art supplies specifically for Project X, but it didn't provide any clear evidence of her involvement in the scheme.

As they continued to search Selena's belongings, they found a folder filled with documents and receipts related to her art career.

Among them was a letter from her father, Lucas Martin, congratulating her on her recent sale to a prestigious art gallery.

The letter was heartfelt and encouraging, but it also hinted at a deeper issue:

I'm so proud of the artist you're becoming, Selena.

But I have to admit, I'm worried about you getting in over your head.

You're taking on too much and it's affecting your work.

I know you're trying to make a name for yourself, but you can't sacrifice your passion and integrity for fame.

Remember why you started creating art in the first place?

This letter suggested that Lucas Martin was aware of Selena's struggles with her art and her relationship with Alan Collins.

Sam's team continued to search for any other receipts or documents that might link Selena to Project X.

They found a folder labeled "Confidential" in Selena's studio, containing a series of invoices and contracts between Collins Inc. and various art galleries and collectors. One invoice in particular caught their attention:

Invoice #123456
Date: 02/20/2023
To: Artistic Vision Gallery
From: Collins Inc.
For: Art Piece #A-001

Amount: $100,000

The invoice suggested that Collins Inc. had sold a fake art piece to the Artistic Vision Gallery, which was owned by a wealthy collector. This could be evidence of Selena's involvement in Project X, but it was unclear whether she was aware of the scheme.

As they continued to review the documents, they found a note from Selena to herself, scribbled in the margins:

I'm so tired of being trapped in this cycle of creating for others.

I want to make something that means something, something that comes from my heart.

But every time I try, I feel like I'm being pulled back in.

I need to find a way out of this. I need to find a way to be true to myself.

This note hinted at Selena's frustration with her role in Project X and her desire to break free from the cycle.

Selena's Notebook

I've been having these strange dreams lately.

Dreams where I'm standing in front of a canvas, surrounded by colors and shapes.

But when I look down, I realize I'm holding a brush, but my hand is shaking uncontrollably.

I've always loved painting, but lately it's been feeling more like a chore than a passion.

I feel like I'm just going through the motions.

I need to find my spark again. I need to find what drives me.

Sam's team continued to investigate Selena's background, searching for any clues that might link her to Project X.

They found a series of emails between Selena and Alan Collins, discussing the sale of several art pieces to various collectors. One email in particular caught their attention:

Dear Selena,

I'm thrilled to hear that your latest piece has been sold to the Smith Collection.

You're really making a name for yourself in the art world.

Best,
Alan

This email suggested that Alan Collins was not only a client of Selena's, but also a mentor or patron of sorts.

It was unclear whether Selena was aware of his true intentions, but it seemed likely that she was involved in Project X at some level.

As they continued to review the emails, they found a note from Selena to herself, scribbled in the margins:

I'm so tired of feeling like I'm just a pawn in someone else's game.

I want to be an artist, not a factory machine. But what choice do I have?

I need to find a way out of this cycle before it's too late.

This note hinted at Selena's growing frustration with her role in Project X and her desire to break free.

Detective Sam Taylor decided to look into Alan Collins's background, searching for any connections to other art scams or schemes.

He discovered that Alan Collins had a history of being involved in several high-profile art scandals, including a major forgery ring in the early 2000s.

Alan Collins's background check also revealed a pattern of using his wealth and influence to silence critics and discredit those who got too close to the truth. It seemed likely that he was involved in Project X, but the extent of his involvement was still unclear.

As Sam continued to dig deeper, he found a series of cryptic notes in Selena's diary, hinting at her growing unease with Alan Collins's behavior:

Selena's Notebook

I'm trapped in a nightmare. Alan is pulling all the strings, and I'm just a puppet.

I need to get out, but I don't know how. I'm too scared to confront him, and I'm too tired to keep running.

I feel like I'm losing myself in all of this. I need to find my voice again.

These notes suggested that Selena was aware of Alan's true nature, but was too afraid to take action.

Detective Sam Taylor decided to look into Alan Collins's financial records to see if there were any suspicious transactions related to Project X.

After obtaining a warrant, they accessed Collins Inc.'s financial database and began to search for any unusual transactions.

As they scrolled through the records, they noticed a series of large transfers from Collins Inc. to various offshore accounts.

The transfers were all under $10,000, but the frequency and consistency of the transactions raised suspicions.

Sam also found a memo from Alan Collins to himself, discussing a "special project" that required "additional funding".

The memo was dated several months ago, and it mentioned that the project was "high-risk, high-reward".

This new information led Sam to suspect that Alan Collins might be involved in something illegal, possibly related to Project X.

But they still needed more evidence before they could make any accusations.

Detective Sam Taylor continued searching for any other evidence of Project X, scouring Selena's studio and office for any clues.

He found a small notebook with several pages of scribbled notes, seemingly written in a hurry.

...have to get out of this toxic situation...can't keep living a lie...need to find a way to expose them...but how?...too much at stake...

The notes hinted at Selena's desperation to escape the situation she was in, but it was unclear what she was referring to.

Sam made a mental note to ask Lucas Martin more questions about his daughter's relationships and acquaintances.

As he continued searching, he found a receipt from an art supply store, dated several months ago.

The receipt listed a large quantity of high-quality canvas and paints, as well as a few unusual items like rare pigments and customized brushes.

Sam wondered if these items might be related to Project X.

He made a note to investigate the art supply store and ask if they had any surveillance footage of Selena making the purchase.

Detective Sam Taylor decided to look into Lucas Martin's financial records to see if he had any connections to Project X.

After obtaining a warrant, they accessed Lucas Martin's financial database and began to search for any unusual transactions.

As they scrolled through the records, they noticed a few large transfers from Lucas Martin's personal account to various art galleries and collectors.

However, none of the transfers seemed suspicious or out of the ordinary.

Sam was about to close the investigation when they noticed a small, almost imperceptible discrepancy in one of the transactions.

It seemed that Lucas Martin had transferred a small amount of money to an account under the name "S.M." - Selena's initials.

This new information raised more questions than answers.

Was Lucas Martin involved in Project X? And if so, what was his relationship with his daughter?

Detective Sam Taylor decided to confront Alan Collins about the suspicious transactions and the memo.

They scheduled a meeting with him at his office, trying to remain impartial and not jump to conclusions.

When they arrived at the office, they were greeted by Alan Collins's assistant, who led them to his office.

Alan Collins was sitting behind his desk, looking calm and collected.

"So, what can I do for you, Detective?" he asked, leaning back in his chair.

"We've been investigating the death of Selena Martin," Sam replied. "And we found some suspicious transactions in your financial records. Can you explain what's going on?"

Alan Collins smiled, his eyes glinting with amusement. "Oh, you're referring to the little 'investment' I made in Artistic Vision Gallery? That was just a... business opportunity I was exploring."

Sam raised an eyebrow. "An investment? That's not how it looks from here. It looks like you're funding fake art sales."

Alan Collins chuckled. "Ah, no. No, no, no. That's not what's happening at all. You're just misunderstanding the situation."

Sam pressed on, sensing that Alan Collins was hiding something. "And what about this memo? The one that mentions a 'special project' requiring 'additional funding'?"

Alan Collins's expression changed, his eyes narrowing slightly. "That? Oh, that was just a... a little side project I was working on. Nothing to worry about."

Sam wasn't buying it. He could tell that Alan Collins was hiding something, but he didn't know what.

Detective Sam Taylor leaned forward; his eyes locked on Alan Collins's. "I'm not buying what you're selling, Alan.

You're not going to get away with hiding the truth. What's really going on with this 'side project' and the memo?"

Alan Collins sighed, his expression growing more tense. "Fine, fine. I'll tell you. But you have to understand that it was just a small, isolated incident. A mistake that's been blown out of proportion."

Sam's instincts told him that Alan Collins was hiding something big, but he decided to keep pushing. "What kind of mistake?"

Alan Collins hesitated before speaking. "I may have... loaned some money to a friend who was struggling to get his art career off the ground. He was working on a new piece, and I thought it had potential. So, I... invested in it."

Sam raised an eyebrow. "A loan? You called it a 'special project' in the memo, not a loan."

Alan Collins's face turned red. "I... I may have misspoken. It was a loan, yes. But it was a special loan, because it was for a very specific purpose."

Sam's gut told him that Alan Collins was hiding something more sinister than just a simple loan gone bad.

He decided to push further.

"What purpose?" Sam asked.

Alan Collins's voice dropped to a whisper. "He was working on a piece for... a very discerning collector. Someone who would pay top dollar for the right artwork."

Sam's mind raced with possibilities.

Was Alan Collins involved in some kind of art fraud scheme?

Was Selena somehow tangled up in it?

Detective Sam Taylor decided to ask Alan Collins about Lucas Martin's involvement in Project X.

"Alan, I know you're trying to downplay the significance of the memo and the 'side project', but I have a feeling that Lucas Martin is more involved than he's letting on," Sam said, his eyes locked on Alan's.

Alan Collins's expression turned guarded. "I don't know what you're talking about, Sam. Lucas Martin is just a concerned father who wants to help his daughter succeed."

Sam raised an eyebrow. "Concerned father? I think you're hiding something, Alan. What is his involvement in Project X?"

Alan Collins sighed, rubbing his temples. "Fine. If you must know, Lucas Martin did approach me with an offer to invest in Project X. He was enthusiastic about the potential for profit and wanted to get involved."

Sam's eyes narrowed. "And what did you tell him?"

"I told him that I was already invested and that he should focus on his own business ventures," Alan Collins replied quickly.

Sam wasn't convinced. He had a feeling that Lucas Martin was more involved than he was letting on.

Detective Sam Taylor sat across from Lucas Martin; his eyes locked on the man's nervous expression.

"Lucas, I know you're involved in Project X," Sam said, his voice firm but controlled. "Alan Collins told me that you approached him with an offer to invest in the project."

Lucas Martin's eyes darted around the room before landing back on Sam. "I... I don't know what you're talking about," he stammered.

Sam pulled out a folder filled with documents and photographs. "Don't play dumb, Lucas. I have evidence that connects you to Project X. Fake art sold to wealthy collectors, and I have a feeling that Selena was involved."

Lucas Martin's face turned pale. "How did you...? How did you find out?"

Sam leaned forward, his eyes never leaving Lucas's face.
"I have a good team, Lucas. They're working around the clock to uncover the truth. Now, tell me about your involvement in Project X."

Lucas Martin took a deep breath before speaking.

"Fine. Yes, I was involved in Project X. But it was just a small investment, and I thought it would be a good way to make some extra money."

Sam raised an eyebrow. "Extra money? You mean besides the millions you've already made from your business ventures?"

Lucas Martin shifted uncomfortably in his seat. "Yes, well, I may have gotten in over my head. But I assure you, it was all just a business deal gone wrong."

Sam's mind racing with possibilities. Was Lucas Martin telling the truth, or was he covering something up?

Detective Sam Taylor decided to investigate the artist who received the loan from Alan Collins.

He went to the artist's studio, a small space in a trendy part of town.

The artist, a tall, thin man with a scruffy beard, answered the door. "Can I help you?" he asked, looking suspicious.

Sam flashed his badge. "I'm Detective Sam Taylor. I'm investigating the death of Selena Martin. I understand you received a loan from Alan Collins to fund your art project."

The artist's eyes narrowed. "What's that got to do with anything?"

Sam pulled out a folder filled with documents. "I'd like to ask you some questions about your project and your relationship with Selena Martin."

The artist sighed and led Sam into his studio. Sam noticed that the space was cluttered with half-finished paintings and sculptures.

"So, what's your project about?" Sam asked.

The artist shrugged. "It's just a piece I'm working on. I don't really talk about my work until it's finished."

Sam's eyes scanned the room, taking in the eclectic mix of art supplies and half-finished pieces. "And what's your connection to Selena Martin?"

The artist hesitated before speaking. "We met at an art gallery opening. She was really into my work, and we started talking. We became friends."

Sam raised an eyebrow. "Friends?"

The artist nodded. "Yeah, we would meet up to talk about art, share our work with each other... That kind of thing."

Sam's gut told him that the artist was hiding something. He decided to press on.

"What can you tell me about Project X?" Sam asked.

The artist's expression changed, his eyes darting around the room before returning to Sam's face. "I don't know what you're talking about," he said quickly.

Sam didn't believe him. He decided to confront the artist about his involvement in Project X.

He sat down across from the artist; his eyes locked on the man's face.

"I know what you're hiding," Sam said, his voice firm but controlled. "You're involved in Project X, aren't you?"

The artist's eyes flickered, and he shifted uncomfortably in his seat. "I don't know what you're talking about," he said, trying to sound innocent.

Sam pulled out a folder filled with documents. "I have proof that you received a large sum of money from Alan Collins, CEO of Collins Inc. And I have reason to believe that this money was part of a scheme to sell fake art to wealthy collectors."

The artist's expression changed, his eyes narrowing. "You can't prove anything," he said, his voice growing defensive.

Sam leaned forward; his eyes intense. "I think you're hiding something. And I think Selena Martin was involved in this scheme with you."

The artist's face paled, and he looked away, unable to meet Sam's gaze.

Detective Sam Taylor decided to investigate the artist further, searching for any clues that might link him to Selena's death.

He spent several hours reviewing the artist's studio, looking for any signs of a struggle or any objects that might have been used to harm Selena.

As he searched, Sam found a small notebook belonging to the artist. He flipped through the pages, looking for any references to Selena or Project X. One entry caught his eye:

I'm getting nervous. Selena's been asking too many questions. I need to make sure she doesn't find out what's going on. I've been watching her, making sure she doesn't suspect anything.

Sam's eyes narrowed. This seemed like more than just a casual acquaintance between the artist and Selena.

He made a mental note to ask the artist more questions about his relationship with Selena.

Detective Sam, quickly looked for some entries in Selena's diary and found something relevant

Selena's Notebook

I've been feeling so overwhelmed lately.

I'm trying to keep up with the demand for my art, but it's hard when you're working with people who don't care about the art itself.

They just care about making money.

I saw the artist at the gallery last night, and he seemed so nervous.

I think he's hiding something. I need to get to the bottom of this...

But then I saw my father at the gallery too.

He looked so sad, like he was carrying a heavy burden.

What is going on with him?

Detective Sam Taylor returned to the artist's studio, determined to get to the bottom of Selena's murder.

He sat down across from the artist, pulling out the notebook entry he had found earlier.

"I think we need to have a talk," Sam said, his eyes serious.

"You wrote in your notebook about Selena asking too many questions and you making sure she doesn't find out what's going on. Can you explain what you mean by that?"

The artist shifted uncomfortably in his seat. "I don't know what you're talking about," he said, trying to sound innocent.

Sam leaned forward; his eyes intense. "Don't play dumb with me. I know you were involved in Project X, selling fake art to rich people. And I know Selena was involved too. What did she find out that made you so nervous?"

The artist's expression changed, his eyes flashing with anger. "I don't know what you're talking about," he repeated, his voice rising.

Sam pulled out a photo of Selena and a piece of fake art. "This is one of the pieces Selena was working on before her death. It's a forgery, isn't it?"

The artist's eyes dropped, and he nodded slowly. "Okay, okay. Yes, it's a fake. But I didn't kill her."

Detective Sam Taylor decided to press the artist for more information. "So, you're saying you didn't kill Selena, but you did know her well enough to be nervous around her.

Did you meet with her father, Lucas Martin, on the day of her death?"

The artist hesitated before speaking. "Yes, I met with him. He came to my studio and we talked about...about Selena's work."

Sam's eyes narrowed. "What did you discuss?"

The artist shrugged. "Just her art, I guess. He was interested in investing in her work."

Sam's mind was racing. Why would Lucas Martin meet another artist and show interest in his daughter's art?

Detective Sam Taylor decided to pay a visit to Lucas Martin, Selena's father.

He arrived at the Martin's mansion, where he was greeted by Lucas himself.

"Can I help you, detective?" Lucas asked, his tone polite but guarded.

"Yes, Mr. Martin," Sam replied. "I'd like to ask you a few questions about your meeting with the artist on the day of your daughter's death."

Lucas's expression changed, and for a moment, Sam thought he saw a glimmer of guilt. "What are you talking about?" Lucas asked, his voice evasive.

Sam pulled out his notes. "According to my information, you met with the artist at his studio on the day of Selena's death. Can you tell me what you discussed?"

Lucas hesitated before speaking. "Yes, I did meet with him. We talked about...about Selena's art. He was interested in investing in her work."

Sam's eyes narrowed. "Investing? That's an interesting word choice. What did you mean by that?"

Lucas shifted uncomfortably in his seat. "I just meant that I wanted to help her career. She was struggling to make ends meet as an artist."

Sam wasn't convinced.

There was something about Lucas's words that didn't add much to the expectation.

Detective Sam Taylor decided to confront Lucas Martin about his involvement in Project X and Selena's death.

He started reading an entry from Selena's diary which says

Selena's Notebook

I'm so angry with my father right now.

He's been pressuring me to create more 'commercial' art, saying it will help me make a living.

But I know it's not what I truly want to do. I feel like he doesn't care about my passion for art, only about making money...

I've been thinking about quitting art altogether and getting a 'real job'.

But then what would I do?

I'm scared of disappointing him, but I'm also scared of losing myself in this world.

Sam asked Lucas about the entry in the diary.

Lucas's expression was clueless.

"Mr. Martin, I've discovered that you were involved in a scheme to sell fake art to rich people through Project X. I need to know if you had any involvement in your daughter's death," Sam said, his tone firm.

Lucas's expression turned cold. "I don't know what you're talking about. Project X was just a business venture, a way for Selena to make a living."

Sam pulled out a photo of Selena's artwork from the project. "This is one of the pieces you were promoting through Project X. It's not her style at all. She was being forced to create fake art, wasn't she?"

Lucas's eyes narrowed. "I don't know what you're talking about. Selena was happy with her work."

Sam's gut told him that Lucas was lying. "I think you're hiding something, Mr. Martin. And I think your daughter knew something about Project X that you didn't want her to share."

Detective Sam Taylor decided to confront Lucas Martin again, this time asking about Alan Collins's involvement in Project X and Selena's death.

"Mr. Martin, I know you're involved in Project X. I want to know if Alan Collins, the CEO of Collins Inc., is also involved," Sam said, his tone firm.

Lucas's expression turned guarded. "I don't know what you're talking about. Alan Collins is just a business partner."

Sam's eyes narrowed. "A business partner who was pushing Selena to create fake art for Project X. I think he had more to do with her death than you're letting on."

Lucas hesitated before speaking. "Alan...he did have some influence over Selena, yes. But I swear, he didn't kill her."

Sam pulled out a photo of Alan Collins from his file. "I think you're hiding something, Mr. Martin. And I think Alan Collins knows more than he's letting on."

Detective Sam Taylor decided to bring the two men together in the same room to see if they would reveal more about their involvement in Project X and Selena's death.

"Mr. Martin, Mr. Collins, I've found some inconsistencies in your alibis for the night of Selena's death. I think it's time we had a chat about what really happened," Sam said, his tone firm.

Lucas Martin shifted uncomfortably in his seat, while Alan Collins leaned back, a smug expression on his face.

"I don't know what you're talking about," Lucas said.

Sam pulled out a photo of Selena's artwork from the project. "This is one of the pieces you were promoting through Project X. It's not her style at all. She was being forced to create fake art, wasn't she?"

Alan Collins snorted. "Forced? Ha! Selena was happy to be a part of Project X. She loved the attention and the money."

Lucas's eyes flashed with anger. "Alan, that's not true. Selena was miserable with Project X. She hated creating fake art."

Sam's eyes locked onto Lucas. "And you knew about it, didn't you? You knew your daughter was being forced to create art that wasn't hers."

Lucas's expression faltered. "I... I didn't know about the details, but I knew she was unhappy."

Sam turned to Alan Collins. "And you, Mr. Collins, how did you benefit from Selena's death?"

Alan Collins shrugged. "I didn't benefit from her death. I just lost a valuable asset."

Detective Sam Taylor decided to bring all three suspects together in one room to continue the investigation.

He called out to the artist who received the loan, Lucas Martin, and Alan Collins, CEO of Collins Inc.

The three men walked into the room, looking nervous and anxious. Sam began by asking Lucas about his involvement in Project X.

"Mr. Martin, can you explain why your daughter was involved in a scheme to sell fake art to rich people?" Sam asked.

Lucas shifted uncomfortably. "I didn't know about it at first. Selena told me she was just helping a friend with a business venture."

Sam turned to the artist. "And you, sir, how did you get involved with Project X?"

The artist hesitated before speaking. "I was struggling to make ends meet as an artist. Alan here offered me a loan to create art for Project X, promising it would be worth a lot of money."

Sam turned to Alan Collins. "And you, Mr. Collins, how did you become involved with this project?"

Alan's expression turned cold. "I saw an opportunity to make a lot of money by selling fake art to rich people who didn't know any better."

Sam's eyes narrowed. "I think you all are hiding something. Let me ask you again: what happened on the night of Selena's death?"

The three men exchanged nervous glances before Lucas spoke up.

"I don't know what happened," he said. "I was with my wife at the time of her death."

The artist shook his head. "I was alone in my studio, working on a new piece."

Alan Collins's expression turned calculating. "I was at a meeting with some investors, discussing the future of Project X."

Sam's gut told him that one of them was lying.

Detective Sam Taylor decided to confront each suspect with evidence from their alibis.

He called out to Lucas Martin, "Mr. Martin, I have evidence that you were not with your wife at the time of Selena's death.

Can you explain why your alibi doesn't match up with the time of death?"

Lucas's eyes widened in surprise. "What are you talking about? I was with my wife at the country club, having dinner. I can produce a receipt and witnesses to back it up."

Sam nodded, taking note of Lucas's response. "I'll need to verify that information, Mr. Martin. And what about you, sir?"

Sam turned to the artist. "Can you explain why your alibi doesn't match up with the time of death?"

The artist shifted uncomfortably. "I... I was working on a new piece in my studio. I didn't notice the time."

Sam raised an eyebrow. "Your studio is on the other side of town. It would've taken you at least 30 minutes to get there from Selena's studio."

The artist hesitated before speaking. "I... I took a taxi."

Sam's eyes narrowed. "And what about you, Mr. Collins?" Sam turned to Alan Collins. "Can you explain why your alibi doesn't match up with the time of death?"

Alan Collins smiled coldly. "I was at a meeting with investors, discussing the future of Project X. I can provide documentation and witness statements to back it up."

Sam's gut told him that one or more of these suspects was lying.

Detective Sam Taylor decided to confront each suspect with evidence of Selena's struggles with Project X.

He called out to Lucas Martin, "Mr. Martin, I have evidence that your daughter was unhappy with her involvement in Project X. Did you know about her struggles?"

Lucas's expression turned stern. "Of course, I knew she was unhappy. But I didn't think it was a big deal. She was just going through a phase."

Sam's eyes narrowed. "A phase? Her diary entries suggest she felt trapped and manipulated by the project. Did you know about her plans to leave Project X?"

Lucas shook his head. "No, I didn't know anything about that. But even if I did, I wouldn't have stopped her. She was an adult, after all."

Sam turned to the artist. "And you, sir? Did you know about Selena's struggles with Project X?"

The artist looked away, avoiding eye contact. "I... I didn't want to get involved in her personal life."

Sam's gut told him that the artist was hiding something.

Detective Sam Taylor decided to confront Alan Collins with evidence of Selena's struggles with Project X.

"I've found some interesting entries in Selena's diary, Mr. Collins," Sam said, pulling out a notebook. "It seems she was unhappy with her involvement in Project X. Did you know about her struggles?"

Alan's expression didn't change. "I knew she was having some doubts, but I thought she'd come around. She was making good money, and we were all making good money."

Sam's eyes narrowed. "Making good money? You're not just talking about the art sales, are you? I have evidence that Selena was aware of the fake art scheme and was planning to leave Project X."

Alan's smirk faltered for a moment before he regained his composure. "I don't know what you're talking about. We were just selling legitimate art pieces to collectors who appreciated them."

Sam pulled out a photo of one of the fake art pieces. "This is one of the pieces Selena mentioned in her diary as being fake. Did you know about this?"

Alan shifted uncomfortably. "I... I didn't know anything about that specific piece, but...I did know that we were stretching the truth a bit to make our art more marketable."

Sam's gut told him that Alan was hiding something big.

Detective Sam Taylor decided to confront each suspect with more evidence and try to get a confession.

He called out to Alan Collins, "Mr. Collins, I have evidence that Selena was planning to expose Project X. Did you know about her plans?"

Alan Collins's expression turned cold. "I don't know what you're talking about. Selena was just a talented artist who happened to be working for me."

Sam pulled out a folder filled with documents. "These are Selena's notes and research on Project X. She discovered that you were selling fake art to rich people, making a profit off of their ignorance. Did you silence her because she threatened to expose the truth?"

Alan Collins's eyes narrowed. "I don't know what you're talking about. I'm just a businessman trying to make a living."

Sam leaned in, his voice firm. "Don't lie to me, Mr. Collins. Selena's diary entries suggest she was afraid of you and the consequences of leaving Project X. Did you use intimidation or coercion to keep her in line?"

Alan Collins's smile was condescending. "You're just trying to frame me for this crime. I have an alibi that proves I was at a meeting with investors at the time of Selena's death."

Sam's gut told him that Alan Collins was hiding something.

Detective Sam Taylor decided to force each suspect and try to get a confession.

He called out to Lucas Martin, "Mr. Martin tell me the truth."

Lucas Martin's eyes narrowed. "I didn't know anything about that. But even if I did, I wouldn't have stopped her. She was an adult, after all."

Sam leaned in, his voice firm. "Don't lie to me, Mr. Martin. Selena's diary entries suggest she felt trapped and manipulated by her involvement in Project X. Did you use your influence to keep her in line?"

Lucas's expression turned cold. "I don't know what you're talking about."

Sam pulled out a folder filled with documents. "These are

Selena's notes and research on Project X. She discovered that you were using the project to make a profit off of her talent. Did you silence her because she threatened to expose the truth?"

Lucas's eyes flashed with anger. "You're just trying to frame me for this crime. I had nothing to do with my daughter's death."

Sam's gut told him that Lucas was hiding something.

Detective Sam Taylor decided to force the remaining two suspects to confess.

He called out to Alan Collins, "Mr. Collins, I know you were involved in Project X. I have evidence that you were using Selena's talents to sell fake art to rich people. Did you silence her because she threatened to expose the truth?"

Alan Collins sneered. "You're just trying to frame me for this crime. I didn't kill anyone."

Sam leaned in, his voice firm. "Don't lie to me, Mr. Collins. Selena's diary entries suggest she was planning to leave the project and expose the truth about Project X. Did you use intimidation or coercion to keep her in line?"

Alan Collins's expression turned cold. "I don't know what you're talking about."

Sam pulled out a folder filled with documents. "These are Selena's notes and research on Project X. She discovered that you were making a profit off of her talent. Did you silence her because she threatened to expose the truth?"

Alan Collins's eyes narrowed. "You're just trying to frame me for this crime."

Sam's gut told him that Alan Collins was hiding something.

Detective Sam Taylor decided to force the artist, who had been working with Selena on Project X, to confess.

"I have reason to believe you were involved with her death". Sam shouted.

The artist's eyes narrowed. "What are you talking about?"

Sam pulled out a folder filled with documents. "These are Selena's notes and research on Project X. She discovered that you were selling fake art to rich people, making a profit off of their ignorance. Did you silence her because she threatened to expose the truth?"

The artist's expression turned defensive. "I don't know what you're talking about. I was just trying to help Selena create something beautiful."

Sam leaned in, his voice firm. "Don't lie to me. Selena's diary entries suggest she was struggling with the moral implications of being involved with Project X. Did you encourage her to continue participating in the project, despite her doubts?"

The artist's eyes dropped, and Sam could sense a hint of guilt.

Detective Sam Taylor continued to press the artist, trying to get a confession. "Come on, I know you were involved in Project X. Selena's diary entries mention how she was struggling with the moral implications of being involved with the project. Did you encourage her to continue participating, despite her doubts?"

The artist looked up, a mix of emotions on their face. "I... I didn't know it was going to be used for something so...so wrong."

Sam's eyes narrowed. "So, you knew what was going on and didn't stop it?"

The artist nodded. "I didn't want to get involved, but...but Alan Collins promised me a career-making opportunity. He said it would be a chance to showcase my talent to the world."

Sam's expression turned skeptical. "And you believed him?"

The artist's voice dropped to a whisper. "I didn't know what else to do. I was desperate for success."

Sam took the artist to a different room and recorded a statement.

Sam's mind was racing. He needed more evidence, but he also knew that the artist's confession was a start.

Sam pulled out the artist's confession and handed it to Alan. "This is a statement from your artist, admitting to being involved in Project X. You're not fooling anyone, Mr. Collins. You were using fake art to make a quick buck off of rich people who didn't care about the authenticity."

Alan's mask began to slip, and Sam could see the desperation creeping in. "I... I didn't mean for things to go that far. I just wanted to make a profit."

Sam's eyes narrowed. "And what about Selena Martin? She was a talented artist, and you used her talent to further your own interests. Did you silence her because she threatened to expose the truth?"

Alan's voice dropped to a whisper. "I... I didn't kill her, Detective. I swear it."

Sam raised an eyebrow. "Then who did? And what was the motive?"

Alan hesitated, and Sam knew he was close to cracking the case.

Detective Sam Taylor led Alan Collins into a separate room, closing the door behind them. "Alright, Mr. Collins, let's get to the truth. I know you're involved in Project X, but I need to know more about your relationship with Selena Martin."

Alan's expression turned calculating, and he leaned back in his chair. "I didn't kill her, Detective. I told you that already."

Sam pulled out a folder containing Selena's notebook and diary entries. "These are Selena's writings. They reveal her struggles with her father's expectations and her desire for independence. Did you know about these feelings?"

Alan's eyes flickered, and for a moment, Sam thought he saw a glimmer of guilt. "No...no, I didn't know."

Sam leaned forward; his eyes locked on Alan's. "I think you did, Mr. Collins. And I think you used Project X as a way to silence her, to keep her from speaking out against you."

Alan's face remained expressionless, but Sam could sense the tension building inside him.

"Tell me about your relationship with Selena," Sam pressed on.

Alan's voice remained calm, but his words were laced with malice. "I knew Selena through my company. She was a talented artist, and I saw potential in her work. I offered her a deal – join Project X, and I'd make sure she became famous."

Sam's gut tightened. "And what did she say to that?"

Alan's smile was cold. "She was hesitant at first, but eventually, she agreed. She was desperate for success, and I promised her the world."

Sam's eyes narrowed. "And what happened after that?"

Alan leaned forward, his eyes glinting with a sinister intensity. "Let's just say...Selena became too good at her job. She started asking too many questions, trying to uncover the truth behind Project X. And when she found out what we were really doing...she had to be silenced."

Sam's mind raced with the implications. He knew he had to get to the bottom of this.

Detective Sam Taylor leaned back in his chair, his eyes never leaving Alan Collins's face. "So, you're saying Selena became too good at her job and had to be silenced?"

Alan's expression remained calm, but Sam could sense a growing unease behind his words. "That's right. She was getting too close to the truth, and I had to take action."

Sam's gut told him that Alan was hiding something, and he needed to push further. "Who did you have in mind to silence her?"

Alan's eyes darted around the room before settling back on Sam. "I... I didn't do it, Detective. I swear."

Sam's eyes narrowed. "Then who did? Was it one of your employees? Someone you knew?"

Alan hesitated before speaking. "I didn't think it was possible, but...I think it was Lucas Martin."

Sam's ears perked up. "Selena's father?"

Alan nodded slowly. "Yes. He's been struggling with the idea of Selena pursuing her own artistic path instead of following in his footsteps. He saw her involvement in Project X as a betrayal."

Sam's mind raced with the implications. He couldn't believe that Selena's father would commit such a heinous crime.

Detective Sam Taylor's eyes never left Alan Collins's face as he spoke. "So, you're saying Lucas Martin was involved in Selena's murder?"

Alan nodded slowly. "Yes, Detective. I didn't want to believe it at first, but...I saw him arguing with her the day before she died. He was furious about her involvement in Project X."

Sam's mind racing with the new information. "And did you see him on the night of her death?"

Alan hesitated before speaking. "No... I didn't see him, but I heard something strange. I was working late in my office, and I heard a noise coming from outside. It sounded like someone was struggling. I thought it was just the wind, but...I went to investigate and saw nothing out of the ordinary."

Sam's eyes narrowed. "And what did you do after that?"

Alan's expression turned guilty. "I didn't do anything. I went back to my office and tried to forget about it. I didn't want to get involved."

Sam's grip on his pen tightened. "You're telling me you didn't investigate further? Didn't try to find out what was going on?"

Alan shook his head. "No, Detective. I didn't want to get entangled in whatever drama was going on between Lucas and Selena."

Sam's eyes bore into Alan's. "You're a CEO of a company involved in a project that was supposed to be top-secret. You're telling me you didn't even bother to investigate a murder that happened under your nose?"

Alan's face reddened. "I'm telling you the truth, Detective! I didn't know what was going on, and I didn't want to get involved."

Sam wasn't convinced. He could sense that Alan was hiding something.

Detective Sam Taylor's eyes never left Alan Collins's face as he spoke. "So, you're saying you didn't investigate further after hearing the noise outside your office that night?"

Alan nodded. "That's right, Detective. I was tired and just wanted to go home. I didn't think it was anything important."

Sam's expression turned skeptical. "You're a CEO of a company involved in a project that was supposed to be top-secret. And you didn't think it was important to investigate a murder that happened under your nose?"

Alan's face reddened. "I'm telling you the truth, Detective! I didn't know what was going on, and I didn't want to get involved."

Sam leaned forward, his eyes piercing. "Alan, I need you to tell me the truth. Did you have any involvement in Selena's murder?"

Alan's eyes darted around the room before settling back on Sam. "No, Detective. I didn't kill her. I swear it."

Sam's grip on his pen tightened. "Then who did? Was it Lucas Martin?"

Alan hesitated before speaking. "I... I don't know, Detective. But I do know one thing - Selena was getting close to uncovering something big. She was asking too many questions and poking her nose into places she shouldn't be."

Sam's eyes narrowed. "What do you mean?"

Alan leaned in closer. "I mean she was getting close to discovering the true purpose of Project X. And I think someone wanted to silence her before she could reveal the truth."

Sam's mind racing with the implications. He needed to get to the bottom of this.

Detective Sam Taylor's eyes never left Alan Collins's face as he spoke. "So, you're saying Selena was getting close to uncovering something big about Project X?"

Alan nodded. "That's right, Detective. She was asking too many questions and poking her nose into places she shouldn't be. I think someone wanted to silence her before she could reveal the truth."

Sam's grip on his pen tightened. "And you're saying you didn't kill her?"

Alan shook his head. "No, Detective. I didn't kill her. But I do know that Lucas Martin was involved in Project X and was getting more and more agitated as Selena got closer to the truth."

Sam's eyes narrowed. "And did you see or hear anything else suspicious that night?"

Alan hesitated before speaking. "Yes, Detective. I saw someone entering Selena's office around 9 pm that night. I didn't recognize the person, but I thought it was strange."

Sam's ears perked up. "Can you describe the person?"

Alan nodded. "Tall, dark hair, wearing a black suit. That's all I saw."

Sam jotted down some notes. "And did you notice anything else unusual?"

Alan thought for a moment before speaking. "Yes, Detective. I heard a noise coming from the office around 10 pm. It sounded like a file being shredded or something being burned."

Sam's eyes lit up. "Did you investigate?"

Alan shook his head. "No, Detective. I didn't think much of it at the time."

Sam's mind racing with the new information. He needed to get to the bottom of this and confront Lucas Martin.

Detective Sam Taylor leaned in closer to Lucas Martin, his eyes locked onto the suspect's. "Listen, Mr. Martin, I know you're hiding something. And I have evidence that suggests you're involved in your daughter's murder."

Lucas's expression turned cold, but he didn't back down. "I've told you everything I know, Detective. I don't know what you're talking about."

Sam pulled out a folder containing the evidence from Alan Collins. "Alan here has come forward with some interesting information. He says he saw someone entering Selena's office around 9 pm that night, and that you were getting more and more agitated as she got closer to the truth."

Lucas snorted. "Alan Collins is a liar. He's just trying to save his own skin."

Sam's eyes narrowed. "Is that so? Then why did Alan provide us with receipts showing that you made several large cash transactions around the time Selena was killed?"

Lucas's face reddened, but he refused to back down. "That's just a coincidence, Detective. I have many business dealings and transactions every day."

Sam pulled out another document. "And what about this? A witness statement from an employee who saw you arguing with Selena just days before her death?"

Lucas's expression faltered for a moment before he regained his composure. "I was just having a discussion with my daughter about her job performance, that's all."

Sam raised an eyebrow. "At 10 pm on a weeknight? With all the lights off in the office?"

Lucas's eyes darted around the room before he spoke again. "I... I was worried about her safety, Detective. She was getting too close to some shady dealings at work."

Sam leaned in closer. "Shady dealings? What kind of shady dealings?"

Lucas hesitated before speaking. "I don't know what you're talking about, Detective."

Sam pulled out one final piece of evidence. "A security camera caught a glimpse of someone entering Selena's office around 9 pm that night. And guess what? It looks suspiciously like you, Mr. Martin."

Lucas's face turned white as he realized he was cornered.

Detective Sam Taylor decided to call Lucas Martin's son, Daniel, and wife, Jasmine, to see if they had any information about their father's involvement in Selena's murder.

Sam knew that often times family members can be a good source of information, and he hoped to get a different perspective on the situation.

Sam dialed the phone and waited for someone to answer. After a few rings, a voice picked up.

"Hello?"

"Hello, is this Daniel Martin?"

"Yes, that's me. Who's calling?"

"I'm Detective Sam Taylor from the police department. I'm investigating the murder of your sister, Selena."

There was a pause on the other end of the line. "I'm listening."

Sam filled Daniel in on the evidence they had found so far and asked if he knew anything about his father's involvement.

Daniel was hesitant at first, but eventually told Sam that his father had been acting suspiciously in the days leading up to Selena's death.

"He's been really stressed out and paranoid," Daniel said. "I think he might have been hiding something."

Sam thanked Daniel for the information and hung up the phone. He then called Jasmine Martin, Lucas's wife.

Jasmine answered on the first ring. "Hello?"

"Hello, Mrs. Martin. I'm Detective Sam Taylor from the police department. I'm investigating the murder of your daughter, Selena."

Jasmine's voice broke as she spoke. "Oh God, what did you find out?"

Sam explained the evidence they had found so far and asked if she knew anything about Lucas's involvement.

Jasmine was adamant that her husband didn't kill their daughter.

"Lucas would never hurt anyone," she said. "He loved Selena like she was his own child."

Sam pressed on, trying to get more information out of her. "Mrs. Martin, I know it's hard to believe, but we have evidence that suggests your husband might have been involved in Selena's death."

Jasmine's voice began to crack. "I don't know what you're talking about. Lucas would never do something like that."

Sam decided to bring Lucas in for further questioning, hoping that he might crack under pressure.

Back at the police station, Sam sat down with Lucas once again.

"Mr. Martin," Sam said firmly. "We've spoken to your son and wife. They both say you've been acting suspiciously and that you're hiding something."

Lucas's face turned red with anger. "They're just trying to protect themselves," he spat.

Sam leaned in closer. "We have evidence that suggests you were involved in Selena's murder. And we're not going to let you get away with it."

Lucas was speechless.

Detective Sam Taylor and his team obtained a search warrant for Lucas Martin's office and residence, hoping to find more evidence of his involvement in Selena's murder.

At the office, they began by searching through Lucas's desk drawers and files.

They found several documents related to a shady business deal that Selena had been investigating, and it seemed that Lucas had been trying to cover up his tracks.

Next, they searched through Selena's files and found a note from her that mentioned she had discovered a massive embezzlement scheme involving Lucas's company.

The note also mentioned that she had planned to confront him about it the night she died.

Sam's team also found a hidden safe in Lucas's office. After cracking the combination, they found a series of cryptic messages and notes that seemed to suggest Lucas had been planning something sinister.

The next stop was Lucas's residence, where they searched through his bedroom and study.

In the study, they found a journal belonging to Lucas, which contained entries that seemed to hint at his growing paranoia and desperation in the days leading up to Selena's death. One entry in particular caught Sam's attention:

I have to silence her before she ruins everything. I can't let her expose me.

Sam knew they had finally found something concrete.

He called for the forensic team to collect the evidence and analyze it further.

As the evidence mounted, Sam was convinced that Lucas Martin was involved in his daughter's murder.

But he still needed to gather more proof to make a solid case against him.

Detective Sam Taylor decided to search Lucas Martin's office and residence for more evidence of his involvement in Selena's murder.

He gathered a team of officers and they began the search.

At the office, they started by going through Lucas's desk drawers and files.

They found a stack of papers with handwritten notes and calculations, but nothing that seemed directly related to Selena's murder.

Next, they searched the computer and found a hidden folder on Lucas's hard drive labeled "Project X".

Inside, they found a series of emails between Lucas and an unknown sender, discussing a top-secret project that was being kept from Selena.

The emails mentioned something about a "meeting" that was supposed to take place at Selena's office on the night she was killed.

The sender was demanding that Lucas attend the meeting, but Lucas seemed hesitant.

Sam's eyes lit up as he read the emails.

This could be the break they needed to crack the case.

The team continued to search the office, finding a small safe in Lucas's desk drawer.

They cracked it open and found a set of keys, a USB drive, and a small notebook.

The notebook had notes about Selena's work on the project, including some cryptic comments about her being close to discovering something important.

The USB drive contained a series of encrypted files, which Sam hoped would reveal more about the project.

At Lucas's residence, they searched his home office and found a hidden room behind a bookshelf.

Inside, they found a collection of documents and files related to the project, including a blueprint for a high-tech device that seemed to be designed for surveillance or espionage.

Sam's team also found a hidden camera in Lucas's office, which had been installed without his knowledge or consent.

It was clear that Lucas had been hiding something, and Sam was determined to find out what.

Back at the station, Sam sat down with his team to analyze the evidence.

They worked tirelessly through the night, trying to decipher the cryptic notes and decode the encrypted files.

As the sun began to rise, Sam finally cracked the code.

The device on the blueprint was designed to hack into secure systems and steal sensitive information. And Selena had been getting close to discovering its true purpose.

It seemed clear that Lucas had killed Selena to silence her before she could reveal his secret.

But Sam still had one more piece of evidence to find before he could prove it in court... may be a confession from Lucas.

Sam returned and thought to confront Lucas to get the confession.

Detective Sam Taylor leaned in closer to Lucas Martin, his eyes locked onto the suspect's. "Look, Mr. Martin, I know you're involved in your daughter's murder. And I have evidence that's going to prove it."

Lucas's expression turned pale, and he glanced around the room nervously. "I... I didn't kill my daughter, Detective. I loved her."

Sam pulled out a photo of Selena's office, showing the security camera footage of Lucas entering the office around 9 pm. "You're not fooling anyone, Mr. Martin. We have proof that you were at the scene of the crime. And we have witnesses who place you at the location around the time Selena was killed."

Lucas's eyes dropped, and he sighed heavily. "Okay, okay...I was there. But I didn't kill her. I was just...I was just trying to stop her from digging up some secrets."

Sam raised an eyebrow. "Secrets? What kind of secrets?"

Lucas hesitated before speaking. "Selena was getting close to uncovering something big at work. Something that could ruin our company's reputation and destroy our family's legacy."

Sam's eyes narrowed. "And what did you do to stop her?"

Lucas's voice dropped to a whisper. "I tried to talk to her, to reason with her. But she wouldn't listen. She was determined to expose whatever it was she thought she knew."

Sam's grip on his pen tightened. "And then what happened?"

Lucas's eyes filled with tears. "I... I lost control, Detective. I didn't mean to hurt her. It just happened."

Sam leaned in closer, his voice firm but controlled. "Tell me everything, Mr. Martin. Every detail. Every motive."

Lucas took a deep breath before speaking.

"I was at Selena's office that night because she had discovered something about Project X... a project that our company had been working on for years, without anyone knowing about it. It was a top-secret project, and Selena had stumbled upon some documents that threatened to expose it."

Sam's expression turned grim. "And what did you do to stop Selena from exposing it?"

Lucas's voice cracked. "I... I tried to reason with her, like I said. But she wouldn't listen. So...so I did what I had to do to protect our company and our family's reputation."

Detective Sam Taylor leaned in closer to Lucas Martin, his eyes locked onto the suspect's. "So, you're saying you killed your own daughter to protect a top-secret project?"

Lucas's expression turned cold, and he nodded slowly. "Yes, Detective. I'm sorry. I didn't mean to hurt her. I just didn't know what else to do."

Sam's grip on his pen tightened. "You're sorry? You're sorry for killing your own flesh and blood?"

Lucas's eyes filled with tears. "I loved Selena, Detective. But I loved our family legacy more. And I knew that if she exposed Project X, it would ruin everything we've worked for."

Sam's eyes widened in shock. "And you were willing to kill your own daughter to keep it a secret?"

Lucas nodded again. "I didn't mean to, Detective. It just happened. Selena found out about the project and threatened to expose it. I tried to reason with her, but she wouldn't listen."

Sam pulled out a photo of Selena's notes from the project.

"Did you know that Selena had written some notes about the project? Notes that could have exposed the truth?"

Lucas's eyes darted towards the photo before he looked away.

"No... I don't know what you're talking about."

Sam's voice turned cold.

"Don't lie, Lucas. We have evidence that Selena had written a paper on the project, detailing about the scam. And we have evidence that you destroyed those notes after Selena's death."

Lucas's eyes snapped back to Sam's. "No...it can't be..."

Sam leaned in closer. "It can't be what?

Lucas's face crumpled as he broke down in tears.

"No... I didn't mean to...I loved Selena...I loved her so much..."

Detective Sam Taylor leaned in closer to Lucas Martin, his eyes locked onto the suspect's tear-stained face.

"I know you're hiding something more, Lucas. I want you to tell me the truth. What did you do with Selena's notes?"

Lucas sniffled and wiped his nose with his sleeve.

"I... I threw them away. I didn't mean to. I just panicked when Selena died and didn't know what to do with the notes."

Sam's eyes narrowed.

"Don't lie to me, Lucas. We have evidence that the notes were shredded and incinerated. You destroyed them to cover your tracks."

Lucas's eyes filled with despair. "No...it can't be...I didn't mean to..."

Sam's eyes filled with a mix of sadness and anger. "It's over, Lucas. It's over. You're going to pay for what you've done."

Detective Sam Taylor's eyes locked onto Lucas Martin's as he read him his rights.

"Lucas Martin, you are under arrest for the murder of your daughter, Selena. You have the right to remain silent, but anything you say can and will be used against you in a court of law..."

Lucas's eyes widened in shock as Sam's words sunk in. He looked around the room, as if searching for an escape or an explanation that would change the course of events.

"...You have the right to an attorney. If you cannot afford an attorney, one will be appointed to you."

Sam handed Lucas a pair of handcuffs, and two uniformed officers stepped forward to take him into custody.

As they led Lucas away, Sam couldn't help but think about the weight of the evidence they had gathered.

The initial evidence points to Alan Collins, the CEO of Project X, being involved in the murder, but it's not him who actually committed the crime. Instead, it was Selena's own father, Lucas Martin.

It's clear that Alan Collins was using Project X as a way to silence Selena, but he didn't actually commit the murder.

He was too busy trying to cover his tracks and protect his own reputation.

It seems like Lucas Martin was struggling with his daughter's independence and her decision to pursue her own artistic path, which conflicted with his own expectations for her.

He saw her involvement in Project X as a betrayal and was furious about it.

The argument between him and Selena on the day before her death suggests that things were escalating between them.

The fact that Alan Collins didn't report the noise he heard outside his office on the night of the murder is suspicious, but it's not enough to implicate him directly in the murder crime.

It seems like he was more concerned about covering his own tracks than actually investigating what happened.

The security footage, the witnesses, the destroyed notes...it all pointed to one conclusion: Lucas Martin was responsible for Selena's murder.

This case has been a wild ride for Detective Sam Taylor as he pieces together the evidence and uncovers the truth.

Meanwhile, Alan Collins, the CEO of the company, was also arrested in the following charges:

1. Involvement in the money laundering scam which includes selling the fake art via Project X to rich people.
2. Using the project to silence Selena Martin and threatening her via messages and mails using user name "Observer".
3. Covering the tracks, evidence tampering and misleading in the investigation.

The detective and team spent the rest of the day preparing for Lucas's and Alan's summons and building their case against them.

As they worked, they couldn't help but think about Selena and the senseless tragedy that had occurred.

The next morning, Lucas Martin and Alan Collins appeared in court, flanked by their lawyer and looking defeated.

The news of their arrest already went viral and there was massive interest in the people to know about the hearing.

Everyone was waiting for the final verdict.

After going through the evidence and listening to the lawyer's argument, the judge read his verdict and their charges loud and clear in the court.

Lucas listened impassively as he was formally charged with Selena's murder, while Alan broke down hearing his relevant charges.

As the hearing concluded, Sam determined to see justice served to Selena.

The mysterious death of Selena Martin is finally solved.

Detective Sam wrote some final notes in his diary and closed the case.

He will always remember this case and is now ready to take up a new challenge.